Aliette Armel

Love, the Painter's Wife, and the Queen of Sheba

Aliette Armel

LOVE, THE PAINTER'S WIFE & THE QUEEN OF SHEBA

TRANSLATED FROM THE FRENCH BY

Alison Anderson

The Toby Press

Love, the Painter's Wife & the Queen of Sheba

First English Language Edition 2004
The Toby Press LLC

P.O. Box 8531, New Milford, CT 06776-8531, USA
& P.O. Box 2455, London W1A 5WY, England
www.tobypress.com

First published as *Le voyage de Bilqîs*
Copyright © 2002 Editions Autrement
All rights reserved
Translation © *The* Toby Press LLC, 2004

ISBN 1-59264-053-2, *hardcover*

A CIP catalogue record for this title is available from the British Library

Typeset in Garamond by Jerusalem Typesetting

Printed and bound in the United States by Thomson-Shore Inc., Michigan

Chapter one

The little courtyard is brimming with sunlight—a blinding light, drowning the space bordered by a high wall with a radiant, crushing white. The air is almost incandescent, melting into a fine vapor. The whiteness is dazzling and shapes merge, become indistinguishable. The walls form an almost perfect square, with no apparent breaks, uniformly smoothed by layers of finely ground whitewash. Reverberation accentuates the hold of the white light, its absence of contrast or color. Shadows at the edge of the walls are only an attenuation of the thick, almost solid light. Nothing is set apart, nothing escapes the void.

A young woman steps into the courtyard and her sudden gesture breaks the uniformity, loosens the hold. As she passes, her silhouette draped in a gold-threaded cloth reveals the dark, narrow opening in the wall, ordinarily hidden from sight. She stands in the opening, and her long, graceful form restores width to the opening, the end of a long corridor that runs between the successive walls of the palace, linking this protected space to the rest of the world.

The air displaced by the movement of her body reaches the red flame-colored tree. Bouquets of corollas tremble lightly in the breath of her passage. The young woman leans against the wall closest to the narrow door, and her white robe blends into the smooth whitewash of the wall. Whiteness regains possession of the space, once again closed upon itself. The young woman looks at the flame tree, how it seeks out shade in the lee of the wall and fresh water from the rivulet, which feeds the basin in the center of the courtyard. Since childhood the contemplation of this flower has comforted her—one glance at the gleaming vigor of its petals is enough to give her strength. It was the gardener's favorite tree; he had come from a faraway country, the same as her mother's, and he had once tended to all the gardens of the palace.

The young woman's sudden entrance surprises the bird perched on the edge of the wall: the hoopoe unfolds its glittering black-tipped feathers, forming a crown for its head, and spreads its broad circular orange-brown wings. Then it gives a little hop, ruffling its wings as if preparing to take flight. But the bird is too tame to feign fear for long. The soft *oop oop* of its song echoes twice, then the courtyard lapses once again into the calm and silence the young queen requires, for this is a refuge from everything and everyone except her own presence, conferring as it does a royal brilliance—even if, at this moment, she would like to be rid of all her titles and decorations.

A gentle breeze refreshes her cheeks; a few drops of sweat pearl on either side of her high forehead beneath the intricate arrangement of her hair. The expert hands of a maid-servant have artfully accentuated the tracing of her eyebrows, so that their fine line emphasizes the brilliance of her gaze and the set of her eyes in her face with its firm, strong cheekbones. Something is disturbing her, causing her lip to tremble and a tear to form at the corner of her eye; fortunately she did not apply too much *khol* with her brush this morning. There is something of childhood's innocence and dismay in her gaze brimming with tears, and this betrays her true age, however dignified her finery might make her seem.

She has gone sixteen times through the solemn gates of the temple of Almaqah to thank their god for having shown her the sun. Year after year she has passed through the sacred portico, first in her father's arms, then firmly guided by his hand, then by his side, careful to keep her head held high to show her neck, in accordance with the strictures of princely bearing that she had been taught. The child and the adolescent princess once trembled with the fear of making a mistake in the order of the offerings or of spilling the seeds that slid back and forth inside the bowl she handed to the priest, Almaqah's watchman. With her arm outstretched, her hand raised above her head, she held an incense burner that contained translucid pearls of incense and myrrh; she was afraid of spilling them onto the ground. She was afraid of the fragile clay figurines, which were given to the celebrant in an alabaster bowl destined to hold the blood of the sacrifice. Only a few feet from where she stood, the servants held back the lambs and ibexes—still alive, bleating and struggling against the ropes that restrained them. She had learned to remain impassive when her maidservants took her walking among the remote palace outbuildings where the animals are raised, and she refused to play with the newborn lambs. She saw the knife of the sacrifice threatening the trembling little pink forms, she saw the blood pouring from them, she heard how they bleated hoarsely with terror, she heard her father's voice raised to celebrate the holocaust: "Praise be to Almaqah!" Then, severe, he would murmur into her ear, "Why did you close your eyes again!"

Her father let no errors escape him. He emphasized every detail, insisted in a few lapidary phrases upon things that should never have been, but he never showed her the right way, the way that would enable her to acquire the proper, confident gestures. He believed in the power of experience. Through her errors she would learn how to avoid making further mistakes. But he had vanished before she had been able to take the measure of his lessons and his knowledge. For a whole year now, there had been no one to stand by her side and ensure the proper order of the rites, no one to keep an account of the violations to the complex ritual. But the eyes of the dead are sharper and more terrible than those of the living. Every night since that first anniversary ceremony without her father she has been waking up with a start from the edge of the stone of sacrifice. She may be a sovereign, but she is still a woman, and ordinarily she does not have the right to go near the stone.

Dressed in his ceremonial robes with their gold and silver tassels, her father is standing next to her. A servant hands him a freshly sharpened knife chosen from the tray where the holy instruments have been laid out. Now the man with the short neat beard, his curly black hair bound by a tight round head-dress—an emblem of his eminence as Mukarrib of Sheba—stares at her with an unsettling insistence. He has always shown a similar determination in her presence. To her questions he often gives no reply other than a mere "because you must," for which there is no appeal. There is nevertheless a gentle touch to his hand as he inclines her head toward the stone of sacrifice and there is pride in the words that accompany his gesture: "You are my only child, and the one to whom I wish to bequeath my kingdom; you have become worthy through the education I have given you, through your ability to receive my teachings and to surpass them. You have a true concern for governance and you respect the gods in whose name we rule. You are just as I have always wished. You will therefore be able to understand the divine law under which I reign and submit to it as I do, however strict it might be." Her cheek touches the stone of sacrifice, and the chill causes her to shiver. The movement wakens her, and she sits up abruptly in her bed. A question, always the same, torments her: *What have I done? What crime have I committed? Why am I the victim of this sacrifice? Why am I condemned to say nothing and to bare my neck for the knife? Why does my father accept this absurd law, why doesn't he use his power to defend me, and hide me? What good is power if it doesn't help us to save the ones we love?*

These questions pursued her until she reached the little courtyard where she has taken refuge this morning, fleeing from the image of another sacrificed body, that of the woman she has condemned to death by the gesture of her own hand. It was to save the lives of others, to be sure! But why should the cost of life be death for another, why is it up to her to judge? She feels so weak—does she not deserve the blade herself, is she not constantly unworthy of her father and his teachings? "I close my lips and remain silent!" is what he repeatedly ordered her. And she cannot keep her lips from opening onto reckless words or to cries she can only restrain by hiding or running away.

She sighs. Her breathing is still strong and quick, but she can barely keep from shaking. With her head against the wall, she wills herself to be calm, but it is as if someone were driving needles into her head. Little wooden pins hold her carefully plaited hair where it spreads fanlike at the back of her head, on either side of her neck. The slightest rubbing causes the little pins to dig into her scalp, and each sudden stab is like a pinch of remorse: *I mustn't lean like this against the wall, it's proof of my weakness, and I'm going to ruin the careful arrangement of my hair. Strands will come loose and fall onto my forehead! That's unthinkably bad grooming. But who am I if I can't even lean my head against a wall? What's the point of being a queen if I can't let someone else take care of things, not even a simple wall! They're asking me to speak for law and justice when I can't even gauge my own abilities. My father is dead, and here am I in the position of a master, yet I haven't even finished my apprenticeship.*

She stands away from the wall, but the sun is already too strong. The air burns like fire. She returns to the shade of the flame tree and, with her palms outspread she takes hold of the end of a branch where a cluster of flowers has bloomed. She presses the bright red petals edged with gold between her fingers, raising them toward the sun like an offering, until the plant resists and prevents her from going any higher; she does not want to tear the flowers from their stem. *Where will I find the strength? From whom can I seek counsel?*

Again she sees the face of the woman who was the cause of her flight, the despair distorting her features. The woman's misfortune was real enough, and unfeigned, but as queen she had been obliged to condemn her, to cut short her life so that the disaster would spread no further.

The women of the tribe of Nasir had come to her to beg for justice: For several years now, not a single newborn had survived among their tribe. All had died of illness before reaching the ritual fortieth day when mother and child were considered strong enough to combat the evil eye and were allowed to leave the house. The infants took sick inside their houses, in their rooms, surrounded by every imaginable protection. Mistresses and servants alike were affected in the same way. As the misfortune spread, they had increased their vigilance. Eventually only those women who had already lost a child during the cursed period were allowed in the presence of mothers who had just given birth. Even grandmothers could no longer help the next generation come into the world! Their traditions were in danger, the cycle of generations had been broken, and the babies continued to die.

One of the child-bearing women was possessed by an evil spirit. This guilty woman was among them and had killed her own child! Shells had been cast, all the ritual sacrifices had been performed—in vain, for the woman was possessed by a demon and had the power to kill defenseless infants with a single glance. And nothing seemed to penetrate the demon's hold, to reveal in whose body, under whose name, he hid. The priests declared that they were powerless—they could not get involved in women's business! They must sort it out for themselves, with their children. The fact that an entire tribe was threatened with extinction was not enough to move them. None of the priests belonged to the Nasir tribe, so they were indifferent to their fate. The royal tribunal was the last resort, and the matter was of the utmost urgency: the next child to be born would be heir to the head of the tribe—it had to survive, to follow in its father's footsteps!

The queen sat on her alabaster throne, raised slightly on a podium, and found herself facing fifteen women. After the customary greetings, she told them to rise. They had put on their finest robes to come to the palace but, in a sign of sadness and mourning, their robes were neither embroidered nor brightly colored. Brown, pale blue, and cream-colored cloth draped their faces and bodies with harmonious sweetness, with something of the grace of childhood. Their bellies, their arms were made to shelter, to welcome, to cherish. Ten of them stood in the front row, five of them slightly behind the others. The serving girls made way for their mistresses, but their anxiety was just as great. There were rumors in the village that the guilty woman was one of them, and that if all the servants were driven away, the problem would be solved. The women of the court of Sheba, sitting on high cushions against the walls all around the room, were vocal in voicing their support: condemn the servants and the evil would be eradicated.

Aware of the power of her gaze, the queen made an effort not to stare at the women of the tribe of Nasir. If only she did not have to use the power that had been granted to her; it frightened and exhausted her. Yet there was no other way. Since the priests refused to help, she was obliged to act on her own.

Tradition held that the queen must never address her petitioners directly. She conveyed her will, or her decisions, through a man of law. Sitting just below her to her right, on a leather seat, he would raise his ear to the queen's lips and, before performing his duty as messenger, would give his opinion and remind her of what was customary. He kept his opinions for his sovereign queen alone and was careful that only she heard what he said. He then faithfully relayed her decisions to the audience, whether those decisions took his advice into account or not.

"The queen desires that each of the ten women who have come before her today speak in turn and look her straight in the eye. Each woman must say her name, that of her father, that of her dead child, and then she should say a blessing for the child about to be born, the child of Nasir's first wife. The queen bids Abîhamad, Nasir's wife, to step to the foot of the podium, before the throne. She will allow her to turn her back to her in order to face her companions and accept their good wishes."

A commotion broke out. The women of the court of Sheba voiced their discontent: "Why should Nasir's wife be honored in this way? Not one of us has ever been allowed to turn our back to the royal throne! The queen is openly flaunting the most sacred customs. Why must the high-born women be subjected to this ordeal? Why don't they just order the servants to speak?"

"Then the servants will be the first to speak." This was the queen's only concession to the women's complaints.

"I am Elzebiah, the daughter of Dhât-Hadran," said the first woman. "My child was named Taher. To you and to your child, worthy wife of Nasir, I wish a long and happy life in the respect of Almaqah."

"My name is Magdhala. My mother died without ever uttering the name of my father, and I did not have time to give my son an identity. May your child, Abîhamad, receive all Almaqah's blessings. May he be placed in his protection—your child, his person, his abilities, his belongings, the clarity of his eyes, and the gratitude of his heart."

There was a tremor in the hall: how could this fatherless child be so insolent, a mere servant who was so bold as to call the wife of the chief of the tribe by her first name! But there came no gesture from the podium to condemn her. The queen refused to name her as the guilty one! The order of the world was indeed threatened now that a woman reigned over Sheba. One after the other the women got up and spoke, mechanically, wearily, reciting invocations that had been learned by heart with varying degrees of success. The queen allowed each woman to say her fill, even if the first exchange of glances was enough. The moment her eyes met the other woman's, she knew whether the spirit of evil was harbored in the woman's body, she knew whether another gaze lurked behind the gaze of a wife and mother.

The queen's interest was aroused by the face of the fifth serving girl. While she had not pulled her hair back as high from her forehead as a princely coiffure would require, her hair was nevertheless held straight back by a veil. In this way the young woman could indicate discreetly that she was not, by birth, destined to be a servant, but that she had been reduced to that condition by misfortune. Her features were strong and symmetrical, untroubled. Her eyes rested for a moment on Nasir's wife, respectful yet not obsequious, then she looked to the throne to catch the queen's gaze. Her expression was sad when she said the name of her dead child, and her voice dropped lower. In blessing the child of Abîhamad she wished for the boy or girl, through the mother's care and example, to be spared the excesses to which an indiscriminate use of power could lead. In her voice the queen could hear the echo of her father's wise precepts when he denounced the abuses of tribal chiefs, using all the dignity of his power to oppose them.

This woman knows, thought the queen, *but she won't say anything. She is indeed fortunate to have such knowledge and be able to stand there with her lips sealed.* The queen raised her hand slightly from the armrest, and with a supple gesture turned her palm toward the sky, reaching out toward the serving girl. She whispered to her counselor: "Don't let that woman leave. When it is all over, you will ask her to come and see me, and to tell her mistress that I wish to take her into my service."

In the hall, everyone held their breath, certain that the guilty woman had been discovered and was about to receive her sentence. Not for a moment did the young woman show any anxiety, nor did she seem at all relieved when the man of law gestured to her to take her seat again among the servants as he called on the first of the tribeswomen.

The fourth woman could not hide her guilt. When she turned to face the unborn child, her demon became apparent.

An unusual brilliance lurked in the woman's gaze, causing it to waver, and the queen detected the demon's presence at once— although this gave her no satisfaction; she was overwhelmed by the task that lay before her. The demon was there, and she would have to force it out, make it known, give it a name. She would have to pit her energy against the demon so that at last the children would be able to live in peace in the tribe of Nasir.

She turned and called on the demon, her voice so loud it caused the entire room to tremble. She forced the woman to lower her eyes on Abîhamad, and to protect the future mother and her child at the same time, she spread one of the colored veils that hung from her shoulder over them and recited the appropriate blessings. The demon spoke: a stranger's voice emerged from the woman's mouth, guttural, broken, as if it belonged to the underworld.

"Mothers must oblige fathers by killing their children. Otherwise the children will kill their fathers, then their mothers, in order to take their place and make their way through life. Infanticide is better than patricide or matricide! It is the well-known law of Wadi Medharran. It must be extended to all the tribes, to all the kingdoms."

"And when human beings have destroyed all the posterity of the servants of Almaqah in this way, who will govern our earth?" asked the queen.

"The god whose name must not be spoken! He will triumph over Almaqah, over all the old gods, and he will be helped in his task by the race to which I belong. There is more pleasure to be found in the entrails of the world than on the highest mountaintops!"

In spite of tradition, the queen continued to talk, trying to convince the demon to return to the wilderness where others like him remained hidden. Such demons escaped whenever a woman was won over by their promises. They invaded her through the child they caused her to bear, and this child would be the first to die. The queen knew she was negotiating in vain, but she wanted to delay the moment of the sentence and hoped to reject the obvious conclusion, the gesture of death necessary to rid the evil from the tribe of Nasir. The woman had to be killed, quickly and immediately, while the demon was still speaking. As long as his voice could be heard, he would not seek refuge elsewhere, in any of the other women present. To delay would cause grave danger to those in the room, all of whom had recoiled from the possessed woman now standing alone in front of the podium.

The queen tried again to provoke the god of darkness to anger the demon and force him to reply, in order to distract his attention. She denounced the god's lack of courage—he could not even reveal his name! The woman now seemed to be shaking with a fit; with each moment her appearance became less human, anger distorting her features, her gestures loose and clumsy, words crowding into her mouth while she was unable to pronounce them. She tried to raise her fist in a vengeful shaking toward the podium, but her body was seized with trembling, and she could raise her arm no higher than her waist. The wretched woman seemed to be begging for her own deliverance. Then the queen made the gesture, the one they had all been waiting for: with her right arm, hand outstretched, she sliced the air from left to right. The guard who stood at the end of the podium with his sword planted proudly before him walked up to the condemned woman so quickly that the blade whistled before anyone saw him leave his post. The head fell at the feet of Abîhamad. The wife of the tribal chief turned to the queen with a triumphant smile. Vibrant cries of joy echoed through the room.

The queen turned away from these untimely displays of emotion. She felt as if she were being forced to look at the head, which now had no body. The face was once again smooth, gone were the grimacing wrinkles, the features had collapsed with despair, and you could see the terror in the wide, staring eyes. The queen watched as a tear welled in each eye, at the edge of the eyelids, as if the woman were crying for her misfortune: *Why could you not set me free without taking my life, why could you not let me live and once again give birth, give life? Why do you let your power go no further than punishment?*

The young queen pressed her hands against her ears to keep from hearing the voice that resonated for her alone. She rose abruptly and tore at the bejeweled cloth, which covered the back of the throne. She could no longer see anything, but she could hear a sort of cacophony: the women's chanting, the guard stomping his feet as he waited for order to return to the council-chamber. Her eyes filled with tears, a mixture of pity and despair. She could not take any more—the role she was forced to play, the knowledge she found impossible to assume, the power that overwhelmed her. She was still a child! Why couldn't they leave her in peace? She was trembling with fear, shivering in spite of the unbearable heat.

She ran from the council-chamber, and in the confusion her departure seemed normal. Yet again she was overcome by the strong emotions against which her father had often warned her: "You must show nothing, above all neither anger nor pity, and never show weakness! You represent the kingdom at every moment of the day, don't ever forget it! I have united several tribes into one nation. For the glory of Almaqah, you must never betray my work!" And now, out of weakness, she had been on the verge of betraying him.

Lost in her thoughts, distraught, the queen sees she is still holding in her hands the clusters of red flowers. A quiet sound startles her: *Oop! Oop!* The hoopoe hops along the edge of the wall, moving back and forth, bobbing its head, and ruffling the feathers of its crown. Then it raises its long curved beak proudly toward the sky—a useless beak in such a place where there is no earth to dig in. And suddenly the little queen bursts out laughing: "I know what this bird reminds me of! He looks like the women of my court who think they're wearing a crown the moment one of them has a more elegant hairstyle than another.

That bird can preen and strut all it likes, everyone knows its long beak is there to dig in the ground for worms and larvae—just the way my councilors and ladies-in-waiting are always digging around in hatred to feed their wars and palace quarrels, and the way they love to see heads roll!"

The hoopoe adorns the little courtyard. It landed there a few months earlier, just after the death of the Mukarrib of Sheba, and it has taken up residence in this peaceful spot where the young woman goes when she seeks refuge and solitude. She discovered the tiny domain many years ago, one day when she was hiding from her nurse's fierce anger. An architect's whim had isolated the empty space between two sections of the wall protecting the palace. The little princess came here often to find solace for her childhood sorrows, to hide her treasures, to escape her ladies-in-waiting. Eventually her father accepted—and made others accept—this need for solitude so unusual in a country where only madmen chose to do without company.

The king quashed the rumors that were circulating: "With a mother like hers, it's normal that the princess would act strangely!" He had a fountain placed there to offer cool, fresh water, and he had the walls made higher to provide more shade. The gardener planted a flame tree there on his own initiative. One unwritten rule prevailed: When the princess disappeared, everyone knew she was in the little courtyard. It was strictly forbidden for anyone to go into the courtyard, particularly at these times. No one ever disturbed her there, but in exchange, her father had made her promise not to let her isolation last "any longer than is necessary to unload the saddle-pack of a dromedary arriving from the South."

The king did not specify how much was to be unloaded from the beast, but it became a code between them: "Well, today there weren't many bags of incense!" he would joke. "That may be, but they were of a better quality," was her ritual reply. The day she didn't come back before sunset he merely said, "I fear there was not room for two dromedaries in the little courtyard, and if you change it into a caravansary we'll have to open it out and place watchmen to avoid accidents!"

Now that she is queen, she continues to respect what her father held to be a proper degree of moderation. At times the women of the palace bring her to order. Even now she hears their rustlings in the entrance to the corridor. This means her peaceful interlude is over, and she will have to return to her place among the courtiers of Sheba, to whom she is as closely bound as they are to her. Once again her role will require her to place a mask of smooth perfection over her face.

With a quick gesture she inspects her hair, the drape of her garments, the fold of her veils, the fastenings of her belts: nothing is out of place. She holds herself erect and walks toward the tiny entryway, leaving the scorching heat of the sun behind her. *Oop! Oop!* cries the hoopoe. "I have to leave soon and have things to tell you—when will you listen?"

The queen turns to look at the bird as it nods its head and ruffles its feathers. No, she's been dreaming: the bird did not speak.

The walls close again around the unbroken blinding white light, after the passage of the queen.

Chapter two

Along silence followed the end of the story, and is marked by the rhythmic crackling of the wood in the fireplace. Silence is not unusual between Piero and Silvia. It has always been part of their way of being together. For some time now the silence has been heavy with unsaid thoughts, with stifled discord, with the prospect of a new departure—postponed for the moment, but threatening nevertheless. This morning, silence has recovered its power as a grave and gentle space, where their thoughts and feelings can flow freely from the experience they have just shared, from the resonance of the images released from Silvia's story.

"I've come to tell you..."

Piero finds it difficult to voice the thoughts he has been preparing for so long. Silvia's story has made them seem less urgent. His departure for Rome is no longer of a pressing nature, and the impatience of the pope's representative now seems to be nothing more than the theatrics of a courtier seeking to flex his muscles and show his power by demanding immediate obedience from a humble artist. In his great goodness and indulgence, His Holiness has requested Piero's contribution, but if the fresco for the papal apartments cannot wait, if the painter's readiness to obey is the only gauge of the excellence of his work, how is one to interpret such an honor?

Nothing is of greater importance than images, the visions that impel the painter's hand, which seek imperatively to exist on paper, on walls, on any support that can be stretched or hung and can receive pencil or pigment, lines and colors. Their multiplicity engenders the fear that they might not all be captured, that something might be forgotten or lost: the queen with her child's face framed by her royal head of hair; the narrow space dazzling with white light where she where she stands dreaming...the council-chamber where she has meted out justice; the proud strutting of the hoopoe; the blazing color of the flame tree; and the mysterious servant whose face beamed with the sort of wisdom that the queen herself coveted: *I know, but I will say nothing.*

When the servant and the queen will be together side by side on the same fresco, there must be no doubt as to the status of the woman who is sovereign and mistress of the other, the counselor who remains in the background but whose indispensable presence supports the entire picture. Foreground, background...The solutions offered by perspective to indicate the relative importance of each situation and figure depend more upon the position of the viewer than upon any perfunctory logic. How would the lady's maid react if she knew that the rules of composition required that she be placed in the foreground, out of step with the main action taking place in the background? So that she does not fill all the space to the front of the picture, an artifice must be found: Piero would like to work on the silence that passes over the face of the confidante. Therefore he cannot show her from behind as he has done in other circumstances, for other figures. He must think; with pencil and ruler in hand, he must draw lines in order to define the young woman's exact position and where to place her face; he must use letters to indicate in alphabetical order, as the composition takes shape, all the points that will go to make up her figure. If from the start he can make a rigorous diagram upon which the figures and shapes will be built, they will come alive for the viewer: can there be any task more important than that of giving perennial life to the works of a creator?

He feels hot now, very hot. When he burst into the room on the ground floor where Silvia stands every morning next to the fireplace, he was clutching his thick wool traveling cloak compulsively in his fingers. As she told her story, he gradually relaxed his grip, his arms relaxed, his cloak fell open. Initially he stood still in the doorway, then gradually, as the story unfolded, his movement began to resemble that of the queen in the small courtyard. He turned toward the wall, but could not lean against it. Imposing pieces of furniture in dark wood, covered with marquetry, take up all the space on this side of the room. They hinder him, they are in his way, and he has no idea what they contain. He was not even consulted regarding their purchase. He is the son of the owner of the house—and sees himself, and is seen—as someone who is passing through. He leaves all the material details to Silvia, with the approval of Piero's mother, Romana, who trusts her, and allows her other daughters-in-law to live as they please, to enjoy their country villas and a social life, which Romana and Silvia quite willingly eschew. They share a taste for the home and domestic affairs, and for the gloom of the inner courtyards.

It was daybreak some time ago, but in this room situated between the inner courtyard and the central hallway of the house the pale winter light scarcely penetrates the high windows opposite the carved wooden furnishings. The fire is the only source of light; its flames gleam and flicker, rich in nuances of red and yellow. Piero is always drawn to the fire like a child. Every morning Silvia places her armchair to the right of the hearth, so that she can make use of the light and the warmth to devote herself to her favorite activity, reading, and still remain facing the doorway, ready to take up the domestic chores, which are her responsibility.

The moment Piero crossed the threshold, on the verge of announcing his departure, she began to read out loud from the pages on her lap. She was quick to forestall him, to prevent him from speaking, as she tossed out the first sentence: "The little courtyard is brimming with sunlight—a blinding light, drowning the space bordered by a high wall with a radiant, crushing white."

The storyteller's voice, warm and luminous, resonated with assurance. Now all of Piero's plans have been disrupted. He has succumbed to her story. The painter quickly recognized the queen, the one that the book of saints, *The Golden Legend,* refers to as the Queen of Sheba; the one Bicci di Lorenzo was meant to portray on the walls of the chapel of Arezzo. Since Bicci's death, the Franciscans have entrusted Piero with the creation of the fresco. Until now, not one of the figures celebrated in the text the monks have asked him to illustrate has aroused his interest in the least: not the empress Helen, nor the impious Chostroes, nor the emperor Constantine. Only the story of the death of Adam inspired a preliminary sketch: the representation of the men assembled in mourning at the dawn of humankind allowed him to study bodies scarcely covered by diaphanous cloths, in various forms of natural perfection, not unlike the antique statues he discovered among the treasures of the court of Ferrara. As for the Queen of Sheba, this nameless woman who had come from an unknown place and spoke as if she were an oracle as she discovered the wood of the cross—she seems totally foreign to him. Until now he has felt incapable of coming up with the slightest proposal to honor the contract he signed to take over Bicci's fresco. As always at moments like this, he envisages flight or distraction, some way of putting things off until later, hence the departure for Rome, where another offer awaits him.

Now Silvia has suddenly enabled him to catch a first glimpse of the queen! She is not yet standing before the wood of the cross, or even before Solomon, but is deep within an interior courtyard, at the heart of a palace with massive walls, in a mysterious kingdom where a hoopoe sings. Now that she exists, the young queen, he must seize the fleeting images without delay. But how can he bring to life the transparent whiteness of that courtyard crushed with sunlight, where incandescence dilutes all shapes? There is so much work to be done. Quickly, quickly, he must go up to his studio, his work awaits!

With an abrupt gesture, Piero wrenches his cloak from his shoulders and almost tears the collar. He cannot gauge the strength of his gestures: his massive build, his broad shoulders, his energetic arms, his thick neck, his rather short legs, well-rooted to the ground—all restrain an energy which, if he is not careful, will burst forth with violence. But then he stops short. Silvia's presence, motionless and silent, makes any improper gesture impossible. He cannot behave crudely before her, particularly now with the gift she has just given him: this inspired story, taken from the book on her lap. She has put down the manuscript and folded her hands across the thick parchment binding, as if to protect it. She looks at Piero with a serene gaze, with the same calm she devotes to her reading. He is aware of the rhythm of her measured breathing. Seated in her chair next to the fireplace, she is the very image of permanence, of the continuity she preserves day after day in this house that Piero so obstinately seeks to flee—only to return, each time. Over her simple day gown, with its square and rising neckline, she has draped a cloth of fine wool, and its blueness enhances her pale eyes and the softness of her skin. Piero is on the verge of rushing over to her, to take her hands made golden by the light of the fire, uncross her wrists, and bring her palms to his face to kiss them.

But the queen in her headdress stands between them: She is there, he can see her. Her hair is drawn straight up from high on her temples, and the skillful hands of her servants have seen that no stray wisps have been allowed to detract from the rigorous curves drawn on either side of the forehead. Some ladies in the courts of the north are similarly coiffed. But how has the queen's hair been braided? In Silvia's story, it was the queen's figure as a whole that appeared before him. With each passing minute, she becomes less and less precise, she has begun to escape him, and this inability to recreate her image is a source of distress, almost physical discomfort. He can sense a tightening in the center of his body. He must reach his studio before the image disappears altogether. If he lingers in this room, made so welcoming and warm by the fire, if he takes the time to offer this peacemaking gesture to the woman he continues to love, he will not forgive himself, and he will not forgive Silvia. He needs to leave, he wants to stay. At the very moment the artist's urgency has called him, he feels a renewed desire for Silvia, drawing him to a place to which he no longer has the time to go. For weeks he has felt incapable, useless, impotent. And it has all come back at once. He finds himself divided by opposing forces. Why is he unable to devote himself to his painting without a struggle, without renunciation? He would like to cry out, to break something, to break away…

"Take off that cloak which hinders you so! Throw it onto the bench, Mario will take care of it! Go up to your studio, I've already taken up too much of your time….But I could not resist the pleasure of reading this text to you. A monk who recently escaped from the lands captured by the Turks brought the manuscript back with him, and Fra Bartolomeo immediately thought of you and the commission his brothers in Arezzo gave you. He passed on to me the pages that have already been translated. Others will follow tomorrow."

Already her words have been lost in the stairway as Piero bounds up the stairs four at a time. He needs no explanations; they're of no use to him in penetrating the mystery with which he is preoccupied: the source, the orientation and the density of the light that will fall upon the faces and lend depth to the space. What does the origin of the story matter in relation to this? What is important is image the story will produce. And besides, if he were to pause, he might be tempted to express his reticence, to spoil the atmosphere, which is once again serene between himself and Silvia. He has been wary of anything that comes from Fra Bartolomeo, and he finds it difficult to tolerate the clergyman's continuous presence. Suddenly, halfway up the steps, Piero pauses in his haste to consider a serious question: what is the queen's name? It seems impossible to portray her without naming her; he needs to address her in order to hold her at the end of his pencil. For an instant he hesitates. Should he shout out, use his voice, so powerful it penetrates the walls, to demand the missing information from Silvia? Should he scramble down the steps again to question her? He heads back down a few steps then thinks better of it and sets off again for the upper stories of the house, where his studio occupies the space beneath the roof. The door slams behind him.

Near the fireplace, still seated in her armchair, Silvia relaxes. Her tension is suddenly released. Her body lets go, curls in upon itself, and surrenders, abandoning the straight, rigid posture to which she is normally constrained by the high back of the chair. She has managed to do it; she has succeeded!

She holds the book close to her, clinging to this tangible object in order to believe. Piero will not leave today, nor even tomorrow. All he can think of now is her, the interest of her story. He will be drawn to her day after day, he will devote himself to his project for Arezzo, far from Rome and its intrigues, and he will stay close to this family to which, through him, she belongs. Silvia did not think she would be able to win such a battle. She's not used to struggling: From her earliest years she has learned to take that which is given, to accept whatever comes, without seeking to influence the ways of the world. And it would take a Franciscan monk, the confessor who was once her tutor, for her to learn the laws of intrigue!

Her very existence is also rooted in the strange and the unusual. Where does she come from? Her rank as an individual among the notables depends, to a great degree, on the answer to this question. When she first arrived in Borgo, she had nothing with which to counter the condemnation she read in the evasive gazes and disapproving scowls of the women of this little town where everything seemed to be everyone else's business. *Where does she come from?* Rumors spread in the guise of an answer, forming a judgment that passed for definitive: it would take all her mother-in-law's firmness and the perfection of her own domestic work to impose her presence. *Where is she from?* She knows nothing of the circumstances surrounding the birth of her body. But she does know where, and with whom, her spirit and her soul came to life.

"I was born in a garden of medicinal herbs and plants," she told Piero on the day God led him to her before the church of Santa Maria della Momentana in Monterchi, "in the presence of a woman who could have been my mother but was not. She looks after the monks and the poor. Like all men and women, I come from God, and my little mother taught me how to approach God by serving those who need help and who have even less than we do. I learned how to do the simplest chores and found I had a certain talent. I soon grasped that it is more efficient to carry out the chores of cleaning, tidying, and gardening in a certain order, that which suits the specific nature of each task. I performed my work so quickly that everyone was truly satisfied, not least of all myself. There was a Franciscan monk who often came to visit from the neighboring convent. He could have been my father, but he was not. He used to be a scholar, a man of letters, before renouncing the complexities of the spirit and of language to devote himself to the way of joy and love, to follow the laws of holy poverty. I have always been drawn to letters, to the words I could see in the prayer books; the monk came one day with a book and taught me to read. I always sought to understand what the priest was saying in his sermon, what was in the texts I read at mass....Fra Bartolomeo spent long hours teaching me to use my mind, to attain creation in the place where God shows us the way to understanding, an understanding that is confused and untidy if one goes no further than the first glance—the one with which most men are satisfied—but which is rich with meaning. And one can catch a glimpse of that meaning only after a long and austere search, a stubborn quest where one must take care not to get lost. I've always devoted an uncommon amount of attention to these labors of the mind. 'Why not?' conceded Fra Bartolomeo reassuring me. 'You are not destined to become a nun! But you must never attach a greater price to books and study than to your neighbor and to the daily tasks that fix you to the earth, to the place where God has put us to carry out his work in the world.' He encouraged me to develop the gifts the God had given me."

This portrait of a singular existence did not discourage Piero, nor did it make him want to flee, and he had no desire to make her give up her books. He tolerated the company of the monk whom the Franciscans, for a reason thatremained obscure, had entrusted with her safekeeping. She discovered a great joy on meeting Piero; her feelings were in sudden turmoil, yet it seemed to be the natural continuum of that for which life had prepared her up until then. He shared with her a taste for study and gave her access to the works he had brought back from his sojourns at courts in distant lands, where he came into contact with those who were searching for and expressing new ideas. She once again found herself in an unusual position, and Fra Bartolomeo, transferred by the order of the Franciscans from the convent at Monterchi to the one at Borgo San Sepolcro, helped her to overcome the obstacles. He delivered her from the fear that her tastes and her ability to learn through books—so contrary to the virtues ordinarily expected of a woman of property—might cause her to stray from the divine way.

He simply advised her to maintain the silence and modesty, which came naturally to her, to persist in her withdrawal and in the confinement of her activities within the intimacy of her conjugal home. The only error would be to seek to exchange or share the subjects of her study with anyone other than Piero. "It is impossible but that offences will come: but woe unto him, through whom they come!" as Christ said. Very quickly Piero's family came to count on her to preserve the influence of the eldest son, her husband, upon the family home. This trust had an effect on the attitude of the bourgeoisie. She was able to obtain the consideration, which her dubious origins had deprived her of. Now her good reputation protects her. What does it matter if the servants see her every morning, sitting by the fire, with a book in the place of handiwork on her lap? No one can find fault with her, no one will view it as anything more than a gentle indulgence whose strangeness is perfectly in keeping with the profession chosen by her husband—provided she refrain, as is fitting, from walking alone in the town, from going into the shops without any formal need to do so, or from showing herself in the window of her house. She has become extremely skilled during her rare but unavoidable visits with the wives of notables, at restricting her conversation to the cares of the household, at allowing the small-town gossip to flow past her, while approving the various viewpoints with a nod of her head. She voices no opinions other than whether two particular fabrics go well together in a dress. She speaks only of the recognition brought by her husband's work and the prosperity of the family's estate. In a corner of the family estate she has arranged the quarters closest to the outbuildings, and there she displays her talent at running a house, her skill in anticipating the requirements of the household—planning the meals, training the servants. Her sisters-in-law are grateful that she has spared them from this obligation: the moment their husbands, who are merchants, leave on their journeys, they retire to their villas in the country—which are, for the household, the source of abundant supplies. "May Silvia make the most of this tranquility in order to fulfill, in peace, the role that God has secretly given her," exhorts Fra Bartolomeo.

But he has no explanation for the absence of a child, for this ordeal that God has inflicted upon their union. It is the only matter for which Silvia finds no calming relief in his presence. After so many long years, the word patience seems to have lost its meaning. How can a woman resign herself to not becoming a mother? And why? Piero shares her worry and her desire. Often, after a few weeks abroad, he tries to find out whether his last passage in Borgo left a trace of hope. Sometimes he hurries back, just to spend a night with her, driven by a premonition or a need he does not express. These brief interludes, when urgency upsets everything and leaves no time even for a single word, trouble her deeply, ravaging her both physically and morally. A certain violence, which Piero carefully restrains the rest of the time, is released in such moments. While he is neither brutal nor aggressive, his gestures lose their tenderness, their calm. Something within him wells up, something she does not know how to define; she is afraid, yet she does not know what causes her fear.

How many times has he gone away since they were wed? Ferrara, Venice, Rimini, Padua. She has grown used to the fact that all the men of the family—Father and herbrothers—rely on her to ensure that Piero fulfills the role in Borgo that is expected of him. The eldest of the family has chosen painting to continue the family fortune; his success must also establish their prestige in the town. And when the Brotherhood of Mercy had commissioned a work from him and were angered by the increasing delays with which Piero was executing the desired Maesta, they turned to the family house, where Piero's father agreed to honor the financial obligations entailed by his son's failings, but he relied on Silvia to provide the explanations and calm their legitimate anger. She understands the doubt thatconstantly torments Piero, the contradictory forces dividing him between the search for lucrative commissions, the support of princes, the need for recognition, the fear of betraying his talent, and the difficulties arising the moment he must create the work expected of him—his impression that the subject is escaping his grasp, or that it will not enable him to show his worth or to display the new dimensions to which painting can aspire. Silvia loves Piero, she understands him, and because she understands him she must accept the very thing that hurts her the most: his perpetual departures.

Yet why after so many years, so many long stays away from Borgo, does Silvia fear so greatly this departure of Piero's for Rome? Why does she feel certain that the court there, with all its tentacles, will destroy him, causing both him and his art to be lost? Or that the interests of power will cause him to forget, as have so many others, that for which he was born: the talent placed in his hands at birth by the will of the Father? Why does she feel so certain that the papal commission is a plot hatched by courtiers banished from Rome who will seek to use Piero as an instrument of vengeance?

She did not wait for Fra Bartolomeo's opinion before forging her own; she only spoke to her confessor about the project in Rome quite late in time, at a point when Piero was already arranging for the messenger to confirm his consent. She found, in Fra Bartolomeo's presence, an unexpected source of help. He did not seem to be surprised, and she discovered that he was violently opposed to the journey. He immediately unveiled a plan of action to Silvia: it was painting, and painting alone, that would compel Piero to stay—he might be absent for a few weeks or months, but only to the nearby town of Arezzo. If he could regain the necessary enthusiasm to undertake the commissioned fresco on the Invention of the Cross, he would be able to stay close to Silvia and the Franciscans, far from Rome and its dangers. And Piero's enthusiasm for his painting now depends mainly upon Silvia, that she might apply her God-given talents in a different way! That she might put together a story, on the basis of the notes taken by a Franciscan monk on a manuscript: the Eastern version of the journey of the Queen of Sheba into the land of Solomon. That she make this story an astonishing one by creating an atmosphere, an ambience, and describing the places that could serve as a background for the painting. In his studio Piero has often been read the texts describing the figure or the scene he is working on.

Such a mission seemed complicated to Silvia, almost extravagant, and not really within her reach. But Fra Bartolomeo left her no time to think or to choose. He brought her the first annotations translated by the monk, along with a few sketches, and gave her his order for the very next day, in the name of God: "You can do far more than you think! In a roundabout way you will, in your fashion, be celebrating the grace of God through Piero's paintings. You have not chosen the path down which God is leading you. You are not master of everything. Have faith, my daughter, and you shall arrive in a different place from where you thought you must go—along the paths of which the Lord alone has the secret."

Fra Bartolomeo did not wait to ask for news. He moved the time of his daily visit forward. Silvia saw his monk's habit by the door and sat up in her chair. He seemed to have no idea of the meaning of the word tired! He did not even leave her the time to express her weariness.

"My daughter, the itinerant monk gave me these few notes for you, and this drawing, which is as hasty and awkward as the previous one. He thanks you for the way in which you have transfigured his poor representation of the queen's torso in the text you entrusted to me yesterday evening. In the land whence he comes, you would have been a great storyteller, even if he finds your tale too Western for his taste. Carry on with your task. Has Piero gone up to his studio? May the Heavens be praised! You must continue; you must follow the path of love in the name of the Father, the Son, and the Holy Spirit."

Silvia receives his blessing; she makes the sign of the cross and lowers her eyes. The Franciscan vanishes the way he came. Near the window, a simple wooden lectern, inclined and with an edge, has been installed sufficiently high for her to write on without effort, as she stands between the light of the fire and the daylight and with no risk of attracting attention from outside. She now places the volume she had on her lap upon the stand. She opens it to a blank page, ready to continue her task.

"*Signora!* Rosita has had to go lie down; since morning she cannot keep down her bad humors. The cook has sent me to to tell you that she won't be able to prepare the carp for luncheon. She'll have to set out the lamb from yesterday that you barely touched....When Rosita is absent there's twice the work. She wanted to warn you so that you could make the necessary arrangements if her illness were to last."

Silvia sighs. The Queen of Sheba did not know how fortunate she was. She knew nothing of the worries that the absence of a kitchen maid could cause in a household! Is it easier to be responsible for the daily life of ten other people than for the salvation of the tribe of Nasir? Silvia stands back from the lectern, squeezes the copybook into a pocket inside her garments, and prepares to make her way down to the kitchen. Before closing it within the book, she glances at the clumsy drawing that Fra Bartolomeo has given her: once again, it is a tree, quite bare of leaves this time; its angular lines suggest it is a tree of thorns.

Chapter three

The little queen is seated at her dressing table. Her hair is now loose but retains the trace of tight tresses as it falls to her shoulders, drawing gentle curls on either side of her forehead. She looks her age, all of sixteen. The scooped neck of her indoor gown reveals her décolleté as far as her shoulders. The sea-green cloth shines faintly with hints of gold, and is so light that it seems almost transparent, enhancing the copper hue of her skin as it catches the light from the torches placed on either side of the dressing table. The young girl at her mirror draws all gazes to her; she is a source of light and gentleness in a shimmer of warm colors.

Three maidservants hurry around her, caressing her, brushing her hair, rubbing ointments into her hands and cheeks, massaging her feet, wrapping her in a cloud of incense. At regular intervals they pick up one of the sculpted stone burners where cubes of resin are kept burning, and with a quick gesture they lift the fine fabrics veiling the queen and hold the small burner close to her skin, allowing her pores to absorb the perfumed vapors directly. They make a few rapid turning movements with the incense burner, utter the usual blessings with a little laugh of joy and pleasure, then quickly close her gown around her again to preserve the scent of the essences.

The queen laughs with them, breathes in the musky odors, tries out the various powders on her palette, and is transformed as she applies the different colors to her face. She changes from a woman of distinction to one who is too violently attractive, then she grows intimidating beneath a mask of thick powders and then shines like a bird of many colors. One by one, she lifts her jewels from their box. She tries on a silver necklace with heavy colored stones, observes the effect produced by a garnet-encrusted bracelet, she fixes earrings with multiple-sculpted and cabled pendants to her ears, she rejects a ring with a cabochon that seems too imposing, then stretches out her fingers to admire the brilliance of a ring with a translucent stone whose multiple facets play with the flickering darts of light from the torch. She experiments, changes, and gathers all the jewels together, paying no heed to the strict laws that govern even the most minor adornments at court.

She loves the way the shapes and colors interact, loves to touch the fabrics—soft, crisp, fluid, or rough; she loves to see how they work together with metal, stone and wood, on her naked skin or on the layers of powder, on her arms, around her long neck or her ankles freed from their laced sandals. Even as a child she loved to sit in this way before her mirror, in the flickering light of the torches—not to satisfy herself with her own image, but to compose it, the way a gardener chooses his plants—acclimatizing, trimming, cutting. She had always found it hard to tolerate the authority of the vigorous woman in charge of the chambermaids—she considered her to be stupid and without taste, appointed by the head of protocol to her position only because she valued order over beauty. Whenever there were official receptions in the evening, this duenna would systematically oppose the young princess's choices, making her remove a glittering object and replace it with a duller one, one which she would claim was better suited to the circumstances. The princess merely wanted to learn, to perfect her knowledge and grasp the principles governing the rules of conduct; each time she was disappointed by the aggressive response the governess gave to her questions, the sole argument being a definitive "that is the way things are done." As a princess she always submitted to her decisions without trying to sway her—but what a lack of imagination reigned in her kingdom. It is with impatience that she now awaits the end of the mourning period, the time when her father's death will seem remote enough for her to appear in public again with her jewels. On that day at last she will be able to impress the court with the unusual combination of color and material most flattering to the wearer, and brush aside the "but that isn't done!" with a gesture that will brook no response. Let that old woman hold her peace or be gone! The little queen looks forward to this revenge. She wants to show the court that she has other gifts besides the lugubrious powers that allow her to mete out justice or give orders to the council; she will insist that a woman's adornment deserves as much attention as issues considered graver and more important.

This evening at her dressing table, she drifts away on her young girl's dreams. Eventually she no longer hears the maidservants' babbling, their comments and allusions to certain rather bold scenes from the ancient feasts carved like memory into the jewelry. She dreams of the evening when she will make herself beautiful for *him,* the man whose name she does not yet know, the young prince with his delicate hands and sharp eyes, his fine nose and strong arms, his clear words; he will be adept at the virile games where the dagger every man wears in his belt is easily flashed; he will also be adept at mental sparring and exchanges of opinion. She cannot marry a man who would not accompany her on a path to wisdom and truth, who would have a limited view of power.

"Power for power's sake alone is without meaning," her father would often insist. "He who has no other aim than to obtain more power, or money to fill his coffers, or jewels for women he no longer even looks at—such a man does not deserve to be king. Power is a means of obtaining something one profoundly believes in—for one's country, for one's people, and as a result, for oneself."

Her feelings for the man who brought her into the world and left her his kingdom remain as complex and confused as the conflicting attitudes between commoner and king. Indeed, he had a profound belief in the uses of power that was unusually idealistic, but he often showed himself to be cynical, vulgar, calculating, and perfectly capable of devising the most underhanded plots; he led his country into bloody wars to eliminate his enemies, but for his daughter he wanted a schoolmaster who would place the value of truth above all others. Thanks to the inspired professor her father chose, the young girl learned to view life as a quest. His teachings showed her that it is not enough to be content with what one sees before one, nor even with what is within reach and within sight: one must take one's distances and step back. He also taught that particularly in regard to the king's actions and deeds, one must equally form unlimited admiration or futile scorn, in order to respect his apparent idiosyncrasies, just as the king conceded his resistance to tradition.

The king accepted the fact that his daughter rejected all the suitors introduced by the noblemen and ladies of the court, whose intentions were rife with strategy and intrigue. The morning after the king's death, the new queen sent envoys to the north, south, east, and west, to bordering or faraway countries, in order to search for a man worthy of ruling the kingdom alongside her. She has been waiting impatiently for the evening when she will greet him at last: Her body trembles at the very evocation of the event; she closes her eyes, feels his hands upon her everywhere, like a caress, she imagines a man with black eyes and untamed curls. His untamed nature will be apparent even through his ceremonial garments. She reaches out her palms, hoping for the contact of another body. A maidservant places in her raised hands a new necklace, a simple branch of coral strung horizontally between two fine gold chains. At the center of the coral branch, in a fold of the substance, lies a pearl of great refinement. Its chalky whiteness stands out against the subtle red of the coral. This is the only necklace which might be appropriate for her first encounter with her beloved. It is simple, light, crafted with studied grace and without ostentation. The maidservant attaches the necklace around her throat, and a gentle languor envelops her.

The queen does not surrender altogether: a part of her remains vigilant, attentive to the subtlest changes in the atmosphere of the room. It is a very big room, with a high ceiling supported by heavy dark wooden beams. From floor to ceiling the walls are covered with a white coating. The royal chamber does not flaunt its wealth: fabrics and objects are carefully locked away in chests and hidden in the recesses built into the walls; they are safe from prying eyes behind sculpted woodwork. The space, almost empty, seems immense. At the center is her bed, a board covered with cushions of all shapes and thicknesses, in which she burrows down, burying herself in sleep. She is protected from the gaze of others by a large white curtain on all four sides. Only the corner where she has her dressing table, next to the entrance and the door that is always hidden behind draped curtains, offers a measure of warmth and intimacy. The walls that surround this special place are covered in pastel fabrics.

With her eyes closed, the queen immediately senses a new presence. Someone is standing by the door, an unmoving figure, with no part in the constant comings and goings of the three laughing, playful maidservants. The woman who has just entered the room makes no sound as she glides across the floor. Her rigid upright posture sends a chill into the atmosphere, reminding the sovereign of the gravity required to lead a kingdom, of the vigilance which is necessary. Since the king's death, a mood of treason has settled over the palace. The queen's life is constantly threatened by shifting alliances and plots. Nour, the maidservant chosen among the women of the tribe of Nasir, has become the indispensable intermediary between the busy world of the councilors and the quarters where the queen retires.

"The messenger has returned, my queen."

"Which one? Where from?"

The queen is delighted, claps her hands impatiently. The event she has so longed for has finally come about. One of her envoys to the faraway courts has discovered the prince she has been dreaming of; Nour has come to announce the imminent arrival of her future husband!

"He has brought Solomon's reply to your embassy: the king of Israel refuses the presents from Sheba and threatens us with war."

The queen's sigh is as deep as her disappointment: she does not wish to awake from her dream to hear about Solomon or, even less, about war—a conduct she refuses to see as human.

"What do the councilors say? What statement are they preparing to make? What have you overheard?"

"They'll make no suggestions. They will let you make a decision, which is bound to be bad. They want war, but dare not declare it. The name of David and the memory of his conquests are still too close. They tremble at the power of his son Solomon. But how can they give up the idea of war, for it is the testing ground of their manly valor and the only opportunity to seize whatever power has thus far been inaccessible. They want you, in your inexperience, to take responsibility for an eventual defeat, so that any unexpected victory might be attributed to their bravery alone, which will then come to the rescue of your unwise and senseless decisions. They hope you will be caught in a trap of errors for which you alone will be responsible. And if they were to find themselves confronted with an army that is too powerful, they would melt away into their own tribes, hoping all the while that the invader will be grateful for their withdrawal. They will not go to war if they are disorganized, but they cannot bring themselves to unite under the banner of a woman. Your father bequeathed his kingdom to you, but the tribesmen do not recognize you as a leader. They don't want to hand you the opportunity to unite them. If you declare war, they'll only come together once they've left all the risks for you and have forced you to plead with them. If you give in to Solomon, if you act as if you're about to submit to the foreign god, they'll rebel in the name of Almaqah: all the tribes will rise up, and it will be the end of the order established in this country by your father and his father before him."

The queen listens to Nour's report, staring all the while at the mirror, where she can see the reflection of the tall maidservant's figure. She does not take her eyes from her own face; before her lady-in-waiting came in, her face held a childlike freshness. With the gradual penetration of Nour's words, a mask has come over her, veiling her features. Her cheeks have tightened with the clenching of her jaws, her gaze has grown harder, the intensity of the effort within her thoughts seems to have sunk her eyes deeper in their sockets. Two creases have formed on her forehead, one of worry, one of responsibility. She is again willful, a sovereign who is meticulous in the exercise of her duties, obliged to expel the child within her. Gradually, her shoulders drop, but she tries to keep her neck tall and straight to maintain a posture worthy of a queen as she masters her emotions. The image she had in mind when she tried on the fine coral jewel no longer suits situation. She needs a heavy silver necklace, which will be assertive and imposing. Without the help of her maidservants she unfastens the fine gold clasp and looks for a last time at the sober, balanced necklace, then puts it down on the table in front of her and raises her eyes again to her image in the mirror. "And yet this is me, too," she sighs. "I am the queen just as I am the child chasing her dreams." A glance at Nour's reflection is enough. The councilor understands her unspoken command: give me your advice.

"You've no choice. You have to face the possibility of war, you cannot let Solomon deliver idle threats. You must reject his ultimatum. The soldiers of Israel know nothing of our desert, and that is a considerable advantage. It is said that Solomon's strength resides in a thousand horse-drawn chariots—can you imagine horses in the desert?"

"When I was a child, we had a gardener who came from a faraway country, and he spoke of horses, but I've never seen one."

"Nor have I. But I've heard that these animals are swift and run gracefully. They can carry, and above all, pull heavy loads, and they're much easier to ride and to command than our camels. But they're also much less hardy. They can't do without water nor can they withstand the heat."

"I cannot declare war."

"Why not?"

"That would be to announce my defeat, to allow myself to be led astray by my so-called councilors; it is just what Solomon wants, that is his plan, for he's refused my cautious presents, my pledge of peace; he has an inordinate liking for the violence taught by his god. He wants to extend his power far beyond the limits a wise man can maintain. So that is necessarily a bad solution."

"But you have everything to gain from a victory!"

"Everything to gain? Do you really think so? War brings nothing but destruction, fire, and death, perhaps for me, but certainly for some of the men who will accompany me or the inhabitants of the towns the armies go through. When you say 'everything,' I see only annihilation and devastation. How can you hope to resort to such an extreme solution?"

"I've observed the behavior of men who set off to fight. I've seen how they come together to defend a cause that is beyond them, and they are capable of taking insane risks, of forgetting themselves in their pursuit of victory, not only of personal glory. War is a noble and necessary endeavor, and it shows who is the bravest and cleverest. And they are not necessarily those who have the greatest physical strength. Have you ever seen a battle?"

"Yes, to my great misfortune. My father insisted that I take part in the operations at the gate of Ma'in. It was out of the question that I carry a bow or a spear or that I wear a flaming garment like my father's, the one in which he led our warriors to victory. I had to stay to the rear and attentively follow the movements of the groups of soldiers, think about the causes for each retreat, and see what I could learn from each victorious advance. At that time I was still convinced, like you, that war was part of the noble and unavoidable duties inseparable from the exercise of royal power. I had already heard how the people bewailed this plague that destroyed their homes, their plantations, their water supply, and their storerooms full of goods brought by caravans. I learned what rationing is, as a result of the destruction of a dam during the war with the tribes in the East. Although I was hardly old enough to understand the meaning of the word 'war,' after a ferocious battle outside the city walls, the wounded were brought into the palace, and for a long time their cries haunted my dreams. But I still thought of war as an inevitable ordeal that must be borne with courage and heroism. If people protested, it was out of ignorance and weak character. And would they not forget everything once the grandiose victory celebrations were underway—with banquets, singing, dancing, and cries of joy to erase the very memory of misfortune, the famine and lack of water, the dead and wounded?

"It was as I stood before the myrrh tree in Ma'in that war suddenly appeared to me as an absolute evil, a destructive force in a pure state, implacable, a threat to everything and everyone, without exception. My observation post was not far from the camp, near a solitary tree at the edge of the plain where the battle was being fought. The tree was dry and bare and stood among the rocks; the main trunk rose up toward the sky in a spiral, and its branches formed a rounded crown. Higher up, where it should have ceased to grow, where it should have been satisfied with the majestic shape it had created, the tree continued to climb vigorously toward the sky. The trunk could again be seen as it broke through into a multitude of smaller branches outspread in a sort of corolla. A second tree was growing on top of the first one, extending it, and you could see the green tips of the young thorns coloring the ends of the branches. On its trunk was the red wound of the resin tree, its bark torn open by a man's knife, but this tree had two lives and stood proud behind its sharp thorns, despite its wounds.

"I was fascinated by the tree and could not take my eyes off it. I had no strength to turn around and look down on the plain where the battle was being fought. I was convinced of the necessity and nobility of war, but this was not enough to quell my apprehensions. I could not bear to see the violent movements, these men clashing, thrusting against each other. I could not bring myself to hope for the death of some to save others: my father, his friends, our men! I could hear shouts, the thud of running feet, the rattling of weapons, metal clanging against metal. Suddenly the guards standing next to me began to shout. One of them grabbed me by the waist, causing me to stumble, and he dragged me back: In one instant the tree with two lives burst into flame and was reduced to nothing more than a crackling fire. A blast of scorching air came over me, my face turned purple, the smell of burning tree was overwhelming. Sparks fell onto my clothes. One of the men who had pulled me back now shook me violently. I recoiled from his pull as much as from the burning ash raining down. War had destroyed the tree—two lives and a crown of thorns were not enough to withstand the destructive madness of men.

"I was seized with a blind fury against my father and the way he ruled. He was using war as a means to rally his men around him. At the bivouac the evening before, he had boasted of his warriors' eagerness to prove their bravery and his cleverness in knowing how to use that to consolidate his glory. This sudden inferno before my eyes showed me the consequences of such a murderous attitude. He was sending them to their death, and they were the purveyors of death. I had always been a good, obedient and attentive child; I was thoughtful and applied my reason, and I might have voiced my opposition out loud, it's true, but in the end I always gave in. But now, in the violence of the battle, my anger knew no bounds. I was filled with rage and everything inside me was crying, No! No! I wanted no part of it. No! I could not accept it. I wanted nothing to do with war. I promised myself that if one day the madness of men brought me to defend my country by force, I would do everything in my power to prevent the return of such madness. And still the arguments in favor of war immediately came to mind. I did not have the right to endanger my honor nor that of the people for whom I was responsible. I did not want to—but did I have the right not to want to endanger them. This powerlessness only accentuated my rage.

"The men escorting me pulled me further away. They made me cross the battlefield. They were walking, running, shoving aside the bodies that had fallen to the ground, and they dragged me along behind them. I could hear moaning, the sound of the death rattle. One wounded soldier clung fast to my skirt, and the guard who was leading me set me free with a thrust of his sword, slicing through my dress and the man's arm. I saw the blood gush from the body as it was thrown to the ground, and the screaming terrified me. The smell of burning flesh was everywhere. There were glowing embers, but the fire spread slowly; there was no wind and the patches of grass were too far apart to really catch fire. The heat of the flames added to the closeness of the air. A damp, oily film settled onto my skin. A rain of brown ash covered my cloak, my arms, my face, and my hair; the smoke was acrid. Everything I touched, breathed, saw, and heard was contaminated by horror. With each step I progressed further into a shapeless, viscous mass. And suddenly I felt paralyzed, incapable of moving my arms and legs. As I stood there, I felt I was being thrown into an abyss, being sucked down by a world that was decomposing. Horrified, I realized I had finally found the answer to the question I had been asking relentlessly for years: what is evil?

"When my nurse forbade me from scooping up handfuls of earth the way the gardener did, or from emptying out the chest of clothing that was in my room, or from running away from the maidservants to the stairway at the other end of the palace that led to the forbidden room, she always gave the same excuse to justify her prohibitions: 'Because it is evil.' In return I would ask her, 'What is evil?' And she would say, 'Be quiet.' My father, on the other hand, advised me to leave my futile preoccupation with the meaning of life to the priests. As for the watchman of Almaqah, to questions on that subject he gave a sibylline response: 'If you turn toward the sun, you will escape the shadow.' Even my tutor was reticent, speaking only of a force that sought to destroy man's capacity to remain wholly and profoundly human, evoking demons and their pernicious deeds, or genies who absconded with a man's mind and led him in the opposite direction from where his own nature should have taken him.

"In the chaos of battle, the reply finally came to me in all its clarity: evil was pain willingly inflicted, from which nothing and no one could escape, neither men, nor the earth, nor trees, nor sky. Faced with evil, I felt totally helpless. I could stop nothing, I could stop only myself. I stood stock still amidst bodies I could no longer see. The guards had left me behind for a moment, and now they came back for me, pulling and pushing without consideration, until finally my legs began once again, mechanically, to walk forward. I followed them.

"We stopped by a wall that crossed the rocky plateau. This was the stone platform my father had pointed out to me that very morning as the goal to reach, the proof of victory. My father was lying on the ground, on a black cloth threaded with gold, and he was covered by his flaming warrior's garment. His face was already white and hollowed, emptied of its essence. A councilor came up to me and bowed deeply. This war I so despised had suddenly and brutally made me queen. I had been raised to the throne before I had even had time to contemplate the idea. I was left without any support, with no one to step in between me and the burden of the decisions I would now be obligated to make. There was no one left against whom I might unleash the rebelliousness that I had felt on the battlefield. I could only turn my rage against myself, because now I was sole mistress of war, as of peace. I was alone in the midst of the tribesmen, and now they were *my* councilors. Despite their sincere mourning, they did not hide their pride: they had shown how brave they were, they were the victors. 'He who dies in combat is fortunate,' they proclaimed as they stood over my father's corpse. 'Nothing can come between him and his glory.' I was left alone with my hatred of blood and fire.

"My father's eyes were closed. He had the implacable look of one who knows. He did not even need to give his orders for me to hear them: 'Be worthy of me, my daughter. Control the harmful emotion one can see on your face, make it hard, steady your gaze, raise your chin, stretch your neck! Your garment is covered not with the filth of battle but with the proof of your courage. Be proud to wear it and accept with dignity the tribute paid to you; receive your inheritance!'

One by one, I took the hands of the councilors who knelt before me, granting them permission to stand. I accepted their tribute and my duty, and I made myself this promise: 'I will bring to Sheba that which my father failed to bring: peace.' So, Nour, it is not the very first obstacle you announce to me today that will make me break my oath."

"But how do you plan to deal with Solomon? Don't you think the time has come when you can no longer avoid war? Must you not, above all, defend yourself, as you have said, defend your honor and that of the people who are your responsibility?"

"No, that time will come only once we have tried everything to avoid war. Tell me about Solomon."

"His renown is even greater than that of his father David. His reputation for wisdom is universal. The messages received from your envoys in the countries to the north, south, east and west all contain the same information: there is only one man who corresponds to the description and the instructions you gave the envoys for their search for the ideal suitor, and that man is Solomon! He appreciates equally military and verbal sparring and considers the word 'truth' to be of an almost equal rank with that of Yahweh, the name given to his god, whom he claims is unique. His ability to solve puzzles has never been equaled. He would be a perfect husband for you because his noble bearing is as great as his intelligence. He does have a beard, that may be his only shortcoming. But of course you cannot think of making him king, since he is a king already, of a glorious land, nor can you become the wife of a man who has already called to his palace hundreds of spouses."

The queen is on the verge of interrupting Nour, to dismiss her in a moment of anger: how dare she compare Solomon to the beloved of her dreams? But she hesitates; she hears her father's words of advice: "An impulse that stems from anger is always a bad one and can lead in exactly the opposite direction from where one seeks to go. Learn to use your impulses wisely by always resolutely taking the path in the opposite direction from the one where your impulse leads you!"

What if Solomon were the man who could complete her education, interrupted by her master's retirement and her father's death? And what if he did hold the key to what was still lacking? Or if his method of governance were in fact appropriate for the tribes she was seeking to unite?

"Are there many tribes in Israel?"

"There are twelve: Judah, Reuben, Gad, Ephraim, Menasseh, Benjamin, Zebulun, Issachar, Asher, Simeon, Naphtali, and Dan."

As she recites this litany, Nour's voice grows rich with an intonation that is both strange and familiar. She adopts the music of the language as it is pronounced in the faraway land where Solomon reigns. The sound of it is sweet to the queen's ear.

"Tell me again," she orders Nour. And images arise from within the words: a plentiful land, green and fertile, where the desert sand lies far beyond the oasis…But then her caution is aroused.

"How can a man whom you say is so wise, who rules over such a fine land—how can he want to go to war?"

"All his acts have one aim: to celebrate the glory of his god, Yahweh, to follow his commandments and make him known to all nations as the only god, creator of the world, and master of life. His religion is nothing like ours: We bow down before Almaqah in fear, we observe a precise ritual to protect ourselves from his vengefulness and claim our victory, but nothing really connects us to the sun, it remains a foreign thing. The god of Israel, however, has established a rule that governs each moment of man's existence. To shelter the ark that contains his precepts and to honor and celebrate him by means of lavish sacrifices, Solomon has built a temple more splendid than anything one can imagine. For Israel, Yahweh possesses the truth. This truth must be made known to all men—for their own good, for their salvation—and it must never be betrayed."

"Even if the price is war against other nations? This god is violent, worse than Almaqah, Athtar and Wadd! Our gods make their presence known through the abundance of our harvests, the victory of our soldiers, and the prosperity of our trade—or else through sandstorms, deadly floods, plague, or the failure of the undertakings with which they have been entrusted. They are merciless if men fail to show their respect, if they happen to err in their gestures of worship. But our gods do not claim to control all of life and the entire universe. They assist the faithful in battle, but the conquests sought in their name are not something they have ordered. They are too indifferent to the fate of mankind to care whether more people begin to worship them or not."

"I'm not sure that indifference is a good thing. Our gods no longer propose any satisfying solutions to the government of our world. We've left behind our desert camps, our tribes are uniting, canals irrigate our plantations and our cities shelter behind walls. Our universe has extended its limits well beyond those of the village or the caravan, from one mountain to the next, one oasis to the next, and men have shown themselves to be profoundly similar but also extremely different. How can they live together? A mechanical respect for rigid rituals can no longer suffice to govern their behavior. Men are in need of new guides to direct their steps."

"Have you secretly converted to their religion, to be so praising of its merits, coming thus to its defense?"

"No, my queen. I am guilty of no betrayal. Although some of my forebears bring me closer to these people of the north: My parents were noble, and wealthy. The caravan that was taking them to my mother's father, who was dying in his kingdom in the south, was attacked by the tribe of Nasir. As I am the child of several lands, I am prepared to listen to words which come from elsewhere. Certain episodes in the history of the kings of Israel, faithfully transmitted by the priests, have their similarities to the most deeply guarded secrets of this palace. Solomon's ancestor was named Abraham, and Yahweh often turned to him as one of his most faithful servants. One day, Yahweh ordered Abraham to take his only son, Isaac, to the top of a mountain to offer him in sacrifice. Despite the fact that everything within him rebelled against such a cruel edict, Abraham yielded to the tradition shared by all our peoples: to submit to the demands of the gods even when they demand that human life be destroyed, to honor the interests of the nation over that of the individual, even if that individual is a child or a close relative. In a land far from Israel, the gods imposed a similar trial on your forebear, King Shubab. He received a message from the gods ordering the sacrifice of his daughter, the young Ishta. She would have to be killed to save her people from a foreign threat, from the man who had come from beyond the seas. Your father was leading an expedition to re-establish the caravan route which Shubab had cut off. Ishta was imprisoned in a cave with two torches, a crust of bread, and a pitcher of water. The sacrifice did not protect Shubab or his people, nor did ill fortune spare the maiden herself—Ishta, your mother. Once the foreigner was victorious and had killed Shubab, he set Ishta free, just before the torches burned out. He decided to wed her—she was very beautiful, and it was a wise move to consolidate his victory in that way, to ally himself with the dynasty reigning over the people of the crossroads where the caravans had to pass. Your father did not realize that in her confinement, demons had taken hold of Ishta's mind, and that he would be obliged to lock her away in a room hidden deep within this palace, a room forbidden even to their own daughter."

"How quickly you have learned all our secrets! But tell me more about the sacrifice of Isaac and what that has to do with my mother's fate."

"Precisely! It was not Isaac's sacrifice, but Abraham's. Though he was devastated that he must use his knife against his only son, Isaac's father Abraham had already begun to raise his arm above the altar when Yahweh sent an angel to stop him. The ordeal to which the father had been subjected was enough. Isaac's life was spared. For the first time, a human life was more important than the blood of sacrifice. A ram was slaughtered in the place of the son—who was an ancestor of the very Solomon who has written to you today. The gods of Shubab seized upon their victim's mind instead of her blood, deceiving both their own followers and the foreigner. The god of Israel, on the other hand, enabled his entire people to discover the meaning of the word mercy. Who is to say Solomon would not behave in a similar fashion toward Sheba? Perhaps he does not want war against your people any more than Yahweh really wanted the sacrifice of Isaac."

"What are the exact words of his message?"

"In Jerusalem your envoy and his retinue presented themselves to the king, with the spices, perfumes, and unguents they had brought as gifts, even finer in quality than those ordinarily bought at such a great price from our merchants for the needs of the Temple. The king refused them with a toss of his hand and said, 'What are these gifts? What God has given me is worth far more than what he has given you, but you are proud of your gifts. Return to your people, we will march against you with invincible armies, and we will chase you from your country; you will be humiliated and debased.'"

The queen examines Solomon's words from every angle: she, too, excels at solving puzzles, at untying the knots of meaning where keys to understanding and fragments of knowledge are concealed. *Although he has been offered valuable gifts that he might use to celebrate the glory of Yahweh in his temple, Solomon asserts that his god will not be bought,* she deliberates in silence. *Anything he accepts will lead to dependency, and Solomon weighs in every thing the part that belongs to the present, and the implications for the future. He scorns the gifts brought by an individual he considers impure and unworthy of consideration. Material gifts are worthless if they are not accompanied by tributes to the god whom Solomon holds to be unique and universal; they even represent a form of violence, to which Solomon responds with the threat of violence.*

The queen shifts her flacons along the dressing table, absently, fingers the jewelry that is within reach, picks up a comb, tries to fix it in her hair, then puts it down again. The maidservants stand by nervously, fearful that her abrupt gestures might damage the fragile glass and the costly jewels. They look to Nour for a nod of approval, then step in to put things out of harm's way, with a frenzy equal to their mistress's. They try to anticipate her gestures, reaching for a fragile object before the royal hand can grasp it. The queen's face betrays no emotion apart from a crease in the corner of her mouth that deepens and then relaxes to the pace of her mind at work, as she seeks to reformulate Solomon's hidden thoughts. She is also troubled by Nour's description of the sacrifice. No one knows about the nightmare that has haunted her since her father's death, the dream that has never come to an end. While she listened to the story of the sacrifice of Isaac, a thought crossed her mind: when she wakes up with a start, she thinks it is to escape the knife. But is it not the hand of the angel she does not allow herself to see upon waking, the hand which would stop her father's hand? She would like to know more about this merciful god.

"There is something we can try. Convene the council."

"Now, this evening?"

"No, you're right.…Wait, yes, now."

"Should you not give it some thought, some time?"

"No, hurry! My decision is made. I have the courage to confront the councilors now, right away. Perhaps I won't have that courage tomorrow. I must seal my decision by making it public."

The queen rises from her dressing table: her face has regained its implacable concentration, the apparent indifference and confidence befitting her role. In the vast white room, everything conspires to grandeur, to exigency, to a surpassing of the self.

Nour rushes about the palace. She will have to make haste to assemble all the councilors. But she does find the time to stop in the small courtyard. She moves silently and quickly in the dark, as if she can see without light. She stands at the edge of the basin and calls, *oop, oop!*

It takes the hoopoe a moment to arrive; its wings are heavy. "You may leave again if you so desire and if the winds are favorable to your journey," says Nour. "Your mission has been accomplished: the queen will soon follow you to Israel."

Chapter four

P iero has not left his attic studio for two days. It is a small room, with a very high ceiling. He stands at the table under the window placed high in the wall beneath the dark wooden beams. His gaze wanders from the sheets of paper spread before him into the distance, to the sky tinted with gray and bistre, winter colors. This corner of the building faces north and the rays of the sun enter at an angle, refracted. Piero likes this subtle, warm light, whose variations follow the flow of the days and the seasons. It is something he can play with: In summer he filters it by draping a veil across the lower half of the window. In this way he can prevent the beams of light from falling directly on his paper and dazzling him, yet still leave the upper part of the window free. Thus the clarity and brilliance of the air—the victory over darkness that is the constant aim of his work—is preserved, for is it not the artist's role to extract the brilliance of color and the transparency of light from the shadow? Is it not the artist's task to restore dignity to man—the dignity threatened by the gloom and fury of hell?

Piero struggles against the darkness in the nave of churches; he paints his frescoes on walls deep in shadow, lit only by a pale, diffuse light that has been transformed by the colors of the stained-glass windows. In the chapels Piero demands to work by the light of numerous torches that are distributed around the room. He hunts down the darkness deep in the fluting of columns and the farthest corners of each wall. But the men and women for whom he creates these paintings will see them only in a dim and deceptive light. He must disregard whatever preferences he may have among his preparatory sketches. In the end he must take into account the natural lighting of the space, and divine beauty and majesty reach out to man, are manifest not to crush him but to lift him toward clarity and truth. In the studio in the evening, the shadows reclaim their rights; Piero lights the torches set in the walls all around the table. He no longer dares use candlesticks upon a work surface that is in the midst of his constant movement. More than once the papers rustling around the flames have caught fire, and he has scorched the wide sleeves of his shirt when his arm has come too near the candelabra in a sudden careless gesture.

Piero stands in a position that would be exhausting to anyone else: He sits on a narrow stool, keeping his balance through the strength of his legs as his upper body leans toward the table. He puts his elbows on the table when he needs to think. He lifts his chest and sits very straight when he is drawing lines on the large sheets of paper he has laid out before him: sketches, drafts, heads whose symmetry he checks with mathematical precision, hands, fragments of ornaments, the first effect made by an assemblage, shadow studies. This morning Piero has been trying to depict the queen's mirror in the corner of a large square room, but the composition seems to elude him. Hard as he tries, he cannot find the angle or viewpoint that would enable him to create a coherent ensemble of the cold vastness of the room, which still contains that intimate corner with the dressing table. With a sudden gesture, he brushes aside the sheet of paper and gathers up the materials he has scattered across the table in as he devised a model: The chalk in the center represents the bed, the pencils form the outline of the walls, the glass inkstand will take the place of the mirror in the corner, and the worn stubs of charcoal can be used to evoke figures leaving small clouds of dust behind them. Abruptly, Piero sits back, almost losing his balance, then sweeps the objects from the center of the table and picks up a sheet of paper. If only he could stand at the entrance to the room, like Nour, to draw the perspective lines using the door frame in order to determine the place and contour of each object and figure, as if he were looking through a window. From time to time Piero's massive form stands stock still, wrapped in a sweeping indoor cloak of thick felt that was once white but has been blackened by lead dust. A faint cloud appears before his face with each breath. It would be easy enough to install a fireplace in the wall, which contains the chimney from the ground floor. But Piero cannot bear the idea of workers in his studio, much less the perpetual comings and goings of servants bringing wood for the fire. The air will remain glacial. Yet he does not protect his hands; when his assistants work with him here, they always complain that their fingers are numb and that they have difficulty moving them. Piero is proud of his robust constitution, of the life overflowing from his depths right to the tips of his fingers. Whatever the season, he retains his skill in handling the tiniest pencil.

It is the evening before his scheduled departure for Rome, and he has dismissed all of his assistants. The studio is empty, as is the entire building, a former warehouse whose enormous size facilitates the packing of the large preparatory material for the frescoes. There are any number of places where Piero can exercise his talent—the eldest of the della Francescas is not without property—but he has grown attached to Borgo. He has never been able to adopt the freedom and carefree attitude of his younger colleagues. He feels bound to succeed, to become one of those painters fought over by the different noble houses, one who will travel from contract to contract, from town to town, but will always return to Borgo, where everyone hopes that he will stay at home and take up the civic duties that are his by right. His wife, Silvia, has been representing him, proof that they do indeed have a home, one that will soon be blessed, or so it is hoped, by a birth.

Under his hand, the queen's face is smooth, it catches the light, and glows with an inner radiance. It gives in order to take, and takes in order to give. At the corner of the young woman's resolute lips, Piero draws a crease, a sign of a burden he is all too familiar with: the heir's duty to enrich the inheritance, to accept his condition in order to surpass it, to go ever further, elevating a father's accomplishments by deploying his own talents. "It is not by blindly copying one's ancestors that one pays the highest tribute!" he often declares to the family friends who are surprised at his choice of profession. Fine phrases like this were not needed in order to convince his father, Benedetto, a man who is not one "to trouble his mind with ideas." His merchant's logic has served Piero's cause: His eldest son may excel in algebra and geometry, but he makes careless errors in the bookkeeping ledgers and spends his time drawing plans, lines, and sketches. Never mind, his brothers will be competent enough to take over the commercial part of the family business. Piero would bring in money from elsewhere; he would explore the new possibility of amassing wealth through means available only to the few who have been blessed with such singular talents. Let him become a painter over whom the princes will fight and to whom the most lucrative commissions will be offered.

For Benedetto the matter is straightforward: Piero has talent. The moment his son voiced his desire to become an artist, Benedetto consulted his friend Antonio di Anghiari, a Borgo painter. Piero was so talented that soon Anghiari had nothing left to teach him. So Piero departed for Florence, where the wealth of the princes was equaled only by the variety of artists. Given the young painter's gifts, Benedetto considers that Piero is bound to succeed; this has been obvious to him from the beginning. To become known and established—that is the foundation of the merchant's trade, the only one he knows. The difficulty lies in assuring a regular supply of the highest quality goods; since Piero supplies his own quality goods, success and prosperity are bound to follow. Piero has tried to convey to his father the endless scheming and intriguing he has encountered, the obstacles strewn across his path, but to no avail. The merchant pays no attention to the difficulties his son encounters or complains of: how to make his way in circles to which he does not belong; how to maintain his artistic standards among the patrons of the arts; the adverse effects produced by his adoption of the innovative trend known as perspective—a movement which even in Florence has numerous detractors. It is not that Benedetto asks his son to be quiet when Piero begins to speak of these topics, but he grows absent, making no effort to understand. Yet he finds it remarkably easy to make a subtle analysis of the struggle for influence among the Camaldule monks, the pope's envoys, and the Florentine administrators. Benedetto was particularly successful in negotiating his position, and that of his family, when the pope handed the town over to Florence. He is astute and skillful where his own affairs are concerned, and he expects his son to do just as well. Yet he has no advice to offer Piero on how to behave at the court of Malatesta, or how to secure that prized commission from hesitant, quarrelsome patrons, commissions that would enable him to live there without financial cares.

Nor can Piero share with his father all the anxiety inherent in his work as a creator. He is paralyzed by all the infighting, which informs the very existence of those who move in influential circles, who have money and power. He cannot paint, he cannot complete the commissions he obtained with such difficulty; he is caught up in an infernal spiral. The constant need to beg for attention, to suffer the same humiliations to which the courtiers are subject, betraying his dignity as an artist and mathematician in order to pursue recognition and money—all of this makes him ill at ease, clouds his vision, prevents him from grasping the "term" he needs to organize a painting into planes, lines, angles, and rays, according to the laws of perspective. The fact that he cannot refuse a commission—even if it means that later he will be incapable of completing it—throws him into a mental turmoil that destroys the freedom, vigor, and clarity of his mind that are all as vital to the unimpeded fecundity of images as they are to the careful disposition of geometrical concepts.

He refuses to be a shopkeeper for his father's sake, to be one of those painters who work out in the open, bartering their paintings to regular customers the way his brothers peddle their leather goods or bolts of cloth. How can he bring his father—a merchant who is proud of what he does and who is universally liked and respected in the town—to understand the point of view of the wealthy and noble humanists whom he must frequent and whose recognition is absolutely vital for his success? Such men have equal scorn for those who work with their hands and those who are involved in commerce, an activity they consider degrading. Artistic creation requires an elevation of the mind, together with the nobility of knowledge, the loftiness of poetry and theology, and a love of the ancient world; such criteria are considered incompatible with the narrow-minded, venal, penny-pinching spirit of a merchant. A true artist should never abase himself by being a shopkeeper, and a true artist would rather go without food and drink than compromise his talent. The reputations of those allowed into the inner circle of a prince or a patron, or in the circles frequented by renowned scholars, are easily built and destroyed. There are men who are only too eager to condemn without appeal, in the turn of a few mortal phrases, those they refer to as "false painters": artists who have neither income nor property, who have been shoved aside by the social jostling for official commissions; men who are obliged to accept "craftsman's work" or find other ways to become well-established, simply to place food on the table and provide decently for their families.

At intellectual gatherings, where courtly and frivolous bantering mingles closely with philosophical debate of the highest nature, Piero has witnessed this type of public execution and dares not speak out, taking refuge behind silence, deeply ashamed of his origins. He manages to procure invitations to forums of this type not only in order to acquire a certain amount of recognition, but also to subject his ideas to the sort of confrontations that are vital for his research. And each time he is surprised at how easily the participants can place the art of language, indiscriminately, at the service of the most venomous conversation or of the most lofty ideas about the nobility of the individual and the grandeur of the human mind. At such gatherings, it is only those who are highly esteemed by society who are allowed to voice ideas that go against the grain of generally accepted opinions. Piero has no power based on such wealth, fame, nobility of origin. What chance has he to make himself heard? Even were he to prove persuasive, the ultimate impact would be more disastrous: he would bring upon himself the inexplicable hatred of those who cannot bear to be proven wrong, those who engage in debate simply to see their own ideas sanctioned and who never attack head on but rather from behind, stealthily.

Thus Piero keeps silent and does not share the questions that are trouble him so: Would it be more degrading to sell his work to a member of the bourgeois who wants nothing more than to decorate his wall and honor his house than to accept a commission where the subject, treatment, materials, and even significance are all dictated by priests, monks, or princes—who may be ignorant and vulgar but who, in any case, intend to make a devious use of art to achieve their political objectives? Is it really so dishonorable to deploy one's talent in the back room of a shop, rather than lay siege to a prince and possibly suffer his rebuffs, remaining ever at the mercy of his changing temperament, while running his errands and attending his receptions in the presence of courtiers who are all too eager to slander and intrigue?

Piero listened to the arguments that Silvia pitted against his departure for Rome as if they were the voice of his own conscience, then he rejected them with a violence that was all the greater for her having reminded him of a certain part of himself. It was as if she had set before him an inner conflict he has been unable to resolve. When Piero flees Borgo it is to ensure that he will not be left behind, but he is ill at ease in the role of a courtier, in the midst of intrigues of no interest to him. When he shuts himself away with his painting, he agonizes over the lost opportunities, but whenever he is at the beck and call of princes—in the anticipation of their good offices—he very quickly begins to feel that he is wasting his time, just as he sits testily through political discussions beyond his scope or interest. Indeed, he has nothing to say about the urgency of a crusade in response to Constantinople falling into the hands of the infidels nor about the most opportune moment to convince the pope of the necessity of such an undertaking. He had let himself be caught up in these struggles for influence and thus was convinced he should go to Rome without further delay, on the basis of a promise of a prestigious commission and of a meeting—at last—with Alberti. In order not to go back on his decision by staying, he stubbornly insisted on leaving. The desire to paint, rekindled by Silvia's story, came not a moment too soon to free him from this dilemma. He found the courage to say, "No, there's nothing urgent about the trip to Rome. No, I cannot simply leave behind the work I have begun in Arezzo." In a split second his art triumphed over every other obligation, and he returned to his studio, to the place he would never leave, if he had the strength.

In two days he has hardly left the room in the attic, and then only to spend the time in Silvia's company, moments of renewed tranquility, to hear the story of the queen unfold from within her book. There is a newfound bliss in his life: he is in the early stages of creating a fresco, here in this house left to him by his father and built by his ancestors; he is enthralled by a story told to him by the woman he has chosen. He must do whatever he can to banish his great regret, the sense of something lacking in his life that nothing can erase: there is no child growing up in the nursery who might, one day, display the gift, the talent, and take up the task begun by his father, his uncles, his grandfather. For several hours Piero stands at his table. Something in him is welling up, fermenting, threatening to burst its bounds. In this, too, he feels torn between multiple ways of being and a multitude of desires. He is convinced of the necessity and the merit of his long interludes spent in immobility and silence, but he only feels truly at ease when he has set to work—lifting heavy weights, feeling the tension in his arms as he raises them to leave color and shape upon the wall, while his breath grows more labored as he pulverizes pigments through holes pierced in cardboard, or climbs up and down the scaffolding—all the hard work that goes into creating a fresco in the cold obscurity of a church and the discomfort of makeshift accommodations far from Borgo. He is always wishing he were different from what he is, and that he were elsewhere.

The lead of the pencil pierces the paper; now the scratch he has made on the queen's long, straight nose cannot be repaired. Despite the thickness of the paper, he can crush the sheet into a ball with the simple pressure of his hand. The unexpected strength of his gesture brings with it the entire stack of papers set on the edge of the big table. In a single instant a good part of his reserve of quality paper has been ruined. The sheets now lie creased and spoiled, they have lost their sheen and can no longer provide the pencil with an alluring surface—flat, smooth, and immaculate, and thick enough to retain the light without reflecting it. As he bends over to pick them up, Piero can feel how stiff he has become. He almost slips from his seat and leans heavily on his right foot to stand up and place the sheets on the table. With ample gestures he sketches a straight, majestic silhouette dressed in a long gown. But beneath the pencil's lead her body remains inert, lifeless, devoid of feminine appeal. Piero cannot imagine the queen's body. He needs to feel the velvet texture of her skin, the roundness of her shoulder, her small waist, the curve of her lower back, the strength of her hips hidden behind her apparent fragility. The queen's body is the exact opposite of Silvia's. Piero's wife is slim and narrow above the waist, while her lower body is fuller, as if designed to bear the child the heavens have thus far refused to give them. As for the queen, she has a full bust, and her firm round breasts strain beneath the light fabric of the gown she wears indoors, in her private quarters. Her black eyes sparkle with life and curiosity but also with impatience, beneath narrow eyebrows which lift toward her forehead. The calm gaze of Piero's wife, on the other hand, seems to enfold everything it beholds in a tranquil blue. Her eyes shelter behind lids that are often half closed, beneath her perfectly arched eyebrows.

Piero puts down his pencil: his fingers ache with other desires. He is regaining sensation in his legs after sitting so long numb and tense at the table to keep his balance. The queen's body needs to exist if it is to be painted, even if it will be hidden beneath one of those heavy gowns that conceal and cover. He cannot be satisfied with one of those models his apprentices have built to display the drape of the clothing. Now Piero tosses his work clothes onto the table. He rushes down the stairs, shoving everything out of his way. He does not need to say, "I'm going out" to the servant who is waiting by the door with his cloak. Silvia has heard him and watches from the window where she stands next to her writing desk. The danger of the trip to Rome has been thwarted, he will stay close to her. But she knows the limits of this closeness, and she knows how he is drawn to his other studio, to that which, and those whom, await him there. She knows, and releases a sigh. She puts her hand to her side, where she feels a sharp twinge every time the other woman comes to mind. Then she squeezes her pen tighter between her fingers: why must each victory be marred by regret and mournfulness?

Chapter five

Aclamor echoes along the walls of the inner court-
yard at the palace. All the councilors are on their feet, fervently
proclaiming the decision they have reached after several hours of
debate: "Yes, let the queen go to Jerusalem, and we shall go with
her!"

So the queen has won. But just as the applause rang out,
she blushed, her eyes filled with tears and, to her utter shame,
her hair came loose from its pins and clips and began to tumble
down her neck. Her appearance seemed to collapse and the
child reemerged from beneath the mask of the queen—a child
desperate finding herself alone in the face of the weakness and
incoherence of men and at having triumphed at a time when she
would have preferred to be preceded and accompanied. She has
won the first battle of diplomacy, of the power of words, the
same battle she will soon wage against Solomon to try to persuade him that he has everything to gain through the exchange
and mutual recognition of gifts. Peacemaking will be sought
through negotiation, a display of charm, and the flow of confident words: this is what the council has decided, at her instiga-
tion. But how is she to succeed at her task if at each stage she is
betrayed by her very self, overcome by her own emotions?

Every time she comes before the council, she dreads the
strength and the will of the men gathered before her. She wants
to believe that they are pursuing a lofty goal with shared deter-

mination; she refuses to believe that it is the pleasure of secret meetings and games of power and manipulation alone that arouses them. When Nour tells her of the alliances that are formed and dissolved beneath the colonnades and on the red-cushioned sofas in the rooms with whitewashed walls, the queen cannot find it within herself to care about these plots devised for no other motive than personal advancement or obtaining more money for an already plentiful coffer. She understands only the path of justice, bound stubbornly forward like a caravan across a desert track. Her father had tried, in vain, to pass on some of his gifts to her, that she might learn the art of manipulation so as to know everything, or to wield strategy and argument to her own personal advantage. To his daughter's utter dismay, he often proved to be false-hearted and ruthless. He was capable of calling a man into his private chambers, showing every sign of a warm and solid friendship, only to have the man condemned the very next day to the worst sort of punishment. He would lavish flattery and friendship on his guest in order to draw out the very information required to condemn him. When she witnessed scenes of this nature, the future queen was unable to contain her indignation, her failure to understand, her despair at being complicit to the betrayal, her tears of protest. She was afraid of what awaited her, afraid that in dealing with these same men, she would be obliged to use similar means of governance.

That night, when the extraordinary council had just decided on the departure of the royal caravan, the queen felt guilty of a similar deceitfulness and abuse of power. Standing before the council, she evoked the memory of her father who had died victorious in combat. She spoke for so long that she began to forget the very meaning of her words; she allowed herself to be carried by the rhythm of her sentences, by the beauty of speech unfolding amid words of both firmness and gentleness, full of charm and, at the same time, threat. She watched the faces before her, saw their relief as she evoked their glorious history, as they were in turn enthralled and made impatient by the prospect of the unknown and the idea of adventure. The men followed the flow of her words as if, in other circumstances, it were the harmony of a lute. Her body, hidden beneath multiple veils, became an instrument of power: the brilliance of her eyes, the way she carried her head straighter than ever, her chest thrusting forward in rhythm to her speech, all became commanding, confident, efficient resources in her struggle to gain their support. The expression on the councilors' faces changed constantly with the emotion the queen sought to arouse in them: captivated, tense, relieved, enthusiastic, approving, subjugated—they forgot the very reasons why, only a few minutes earlier, they had sought to abstain, to refuse to opt for or against war, to try and catch her in the trap of her own inexperience. Her words shaped their minds. The weakness of their resistance became almost palpable. Suddenly, there was a commotion: "Yes, that's what we want: Let the queen go to Jerusalem and we shall go with her! We will escort her." The men rose to their feet to assert their agreement and confirm her victory.

But how much value should she ascribe to their support, based as it is upon fleeting impressions, and the ease with which she has convinced them. Will they adopt a contrary position the moment she lets go and turns her attention elsewhere? To what degree can she trust these men whose judgment vacillates according to the general opinion? How much support dare she hope for from councilors who do not have the courage of their convictions, who prefer to conspire in secret rather than express their opposition out in the open? Their weakness disgusts her: She knows they will abandon her, while at the same time they will demand that she renounce her own weaknesses and surpass her own abilities. She sees treachery everywhere and there is no one at her side to lend support., She has sought in vain to find one councilor among all those gathered there who she might recognize as a guide, a man who would be implacable and yet full of tenderness, firm in his self-confidence. If her father were there before her, he would have opposed her with the strength of a simple "no." He would hardly have needed to list the reasons for his refusal; she would have accepted them, and she would have followed him—whereas today it is she who has inspired the men to follow her.

Her head covered with a veil, she glides along the corridors. The courtiers and servants who see her go by have no time to recognize her. She walks so quickly that her steps take her to a place she ordinarily does not allow herself to go, a place of suffering. As she hurries around the courtyard that separates the ceremonial building from the royal residence, she begins to weep. She is running from herself along a vast corridor, down the labyrinth of interconnected passages, which protect the palace from the outside. She is melting into the shadows that cover everything with nightfall and hides from torchlight, refusing to have her way lit by flames. Shocked by her own strength and resolve, she cries out with fright; the victory is hers, but it has also confirmed that she is utterly alone amid all the men gathered there. Who will come to her help when she reaches her own limits?

To her unspoken question comes a silent reply: *Solomon.* Her decision to set out to Jerusalem is driven by more than political considerations—it is inspired by the emotion she felt as she listened to Nour's description of the man from Jerusalem, the son of David and king of Israel—because the description matches her dreams. His wisdom enables Solomon to resolve the most complex puzzles; his experience of a glorious kingdom allows him to find skillful solutions to the most delicate issues of government. But does she have the right to lead her people into an expedition only to resolve what are her own most intimate preoccupations? But such scruples no longer apply; she cannot turn back now. Her resolution is a public matter and is irreversible: her departure is a matter of state. She weeps with exhaustion because she does not have the right to be weak, but weakness exacerbates her weeping. Overwhelmed by emotion, she cannot find the self-control her father insisted upon: "Take hold of yourself, daughter! You must never forget that you are the queen and that it is the dignity of the realm which, at every moment, can be read upon your face and in the rigor of your conduct."

In this moment of anguish, she feels surprisingly close to the hidden woman. She is the queen, the supreme ruler of this country and this palace: no one can forbid her access to the secret apartments. And yet her fear of being seen and the impression that she is committing a crime both persist. She hides beneath her veils, skims the walls, and hastens her step. She enters the royal house. She does not enter through the main door or the majestic staircase that leads to the splendid reception hall beneath the roof, but through a small opening, which is always locked and kept in darkness. After an initial gesture to stop her, the guard hurries to turn the key. Once she is in, he immediately closes the door again with trembling hands.

She climbs the steep stairway, lowering her gaze instinctively before the first step: she remembers that because of the way the place has been built one cannot stand upright without bumping one's head on the hard thick stone. By the time she reaches the second floor, she is out of breath, and here she slows her pace.

Now she can hear the shrill sound of the lament: *"Oh...ou...mi... nyan...gan...ti..."* The sound is muffled by the stone, yet it echoes and mingles with other sounds, confused. It is coming from above. From the outside no one would even know there was a floor there: the irregular steps on the grand staircase make it impossible to detect the difference in levels between the second and third floors. The windows, too, are placed unevenly along the façade, which further hides the few discreet openings not emphasized by any white coating, and which are hidden by pieces of thick colorless alabaster.

The hidden stairway ends on a landing where another guard stands watch by the light of a torch. Shadows cover his face with a mask whose features are darkened and drawn downward, in shame and sadness. The queen stoops to cross the threshold. When she stands upright again she finds herself in the gloomy chamber that seems unchanged since her last visit. Drawn to the main source of light, her gaze shifts to the opposite end of the room. There is a fire on the altar, which is shaped like a round tower. An old woman stands before the altar, mindless of the armchair placed behind her. The benches that surround the room have not been used in a long time. The wall nearest the fireplace is covered with streaks of smoke and with yellow, orange, and red flashes, a sort of funereal dance, unending, spasmodic. The thin torches placed in heavy iron rings fastened to the walls on either side give off a dim glow, illuminating only the faded cloth and a few copper trays stand on their carved wooden feet, on which there are no longer any glasses or pitchers of fresh water: the rules of hospitality have vanished from here long ago.

The old woman has lost weight and grown even weaker, although even at the last visit it looked as though she was about to disappear. It is only through some miracle that her frail legs, which are visible beneath the edge of a wrinkled gown that no longer reaches the floor, carry her deformed, broken body. She can no longer stand straight, but leans heavily to the left. She moves with a bizarre shuffle, devoid of rhythm or grace, lifting first one leg, then the other, as if she were about to topple over, as if something were hurting her, burning the soles of her feet. She chants in a voice that has lost all color, shrill, and grating, a voice so loud it is almost a shout, disturbing and aggressive. Her lament is a hackneyed tune without melody, with words that have lost all meaning until they have faded to traces of an unknown language.

"Mother!"

How did the young queen find the strength to call her by this name? It has not crossed her lips for many years. When, as a child, she would rush toward her, shouting "Mother!" her mother would grimace, and from the way she recoiled and shuddered, the little girl understood it would be better not to voice these two syllables that elicited a reaction of such displeasure. But when she spoke to her in secret, in her games or when she was about to fall asleep, she would continue to murmur her name: *Mother*. One day, she went without warning to her mother's chambers, thinking only of telling her, as quickly as possible, about an achievement that fills her with pride: "Mother, I can read Almaqah's name, and I've even managed to carve the letters onto a wooden stick!"

Her mother whirled around to face her with a barely restrained violence, her voice hissing with a tremor of hatred: "You carve Almaqah's name! You dare to call me Mother! Are you trying to hound me, to pursue and hurt me at all costs? When I cried 'Mother!' from the depths of the cave where my father had walled me up—no one came! No one deserves to be called 'Mother,' ever. Mothers think of only one thing: how to abandon their children and be rid of that burden. You should never have been born, no more than I should have been born. I gave birth by mistake—don't remind me of that. I was cursed, abandoned by the gods, and so are you, just like me. Nothing can ever free you from this curse. What do you mean, 'carving the names of the gods'? Do you wish to arouse their anger yet again? Who is it you wish to mock? How dare you come sneering at me in my chambers, calling me Mother!"

Before the demons had absconded with her mind, there had been a time when Ishta had tried to be a mother. She held the baby, the little princess, in her arms. Standing at the side of her husband, the Mukarrib of Sheba, she showed the infant to the crowd. They had stood at the top of the stairway overlooking the courtyard, and on that day she had looked happy— Ishta, the young mother, proud to be the wife of the king who had saved her and her people from the vengeance of the gods.

The nurse often told the little princess the story of how she was presented to the people of Sheba—a brief moment of glory and happiness. Before long, Ishta ceased to display any motherly behavior toward her daughter, rejecting the child's impetuous affection and showering her with reproaches about a past that did not concern her, yet making ever more contradictory demands. She wanted her exclusive attention, she told stories that took place in the faraway land where she was born, terrible stories of death and torture and child sacrifice. At times, when her daughter was brought to her, she would remain prostrate for a few moments, then she would shout and demand answers to questions the child could scarcely articulate "Why? Why? Why?" she would say, over and over.

"Why what?" asked the child one day.

"How dare you burden me in this way?" shouted the mother, her eyes full of a destructive fury. "How dare you talk back with these questions that are destroying me?" A bowl of burning embers was kept on the altar of her ancestors' gods. She lifted it over her child's head, menacingly. The bowl spilled, and although the child was not hurt, the room caught fire.

The little girl ran away from the "floor of screams," yet she would return, time and again, fascinated, driven by a secret hope: Perhaps today would be different from the previous day. Perhaps her mother would walk toward her with a gentle smile and take her in her arms, murmuring the name she had given her, a name she loved. Her father had called her Bilqis, the one who is both *bal*, an imploration, and *qais*, strength and power—meaning one who is betrothed to power yet will never betray the sanctity of prayer. But Bilqis had become a forbidden name, proscribed and taboo. The woman who came from the faraway lands, whom the little princess no longer dared to call Mother, who never recovered from her wounds, who lived in a world of perpetual fear—refused to use her daughter's name. For her it echoed another word in her language, meaning concubine.

"Your father called you Bilqis to take revenge on me. Let no one utter that name before me, ever!"

In her delirium, Ishta accused her husband of wanting to brand their daughter with the infamy she herself had refused at the cost of her reason. Madness had been the only way for her to escape her humiliation, when the king had decided to bring a new wife to his palace. It was at that moment that Ishta brandished the fiery burner like a weapon for the second time and threatened the palace, and Bilqis stopped being called by her name. Other rumors had reinforced the reasons for silencing the name:. It was said that demons, having possessed the mother's mind, were now hoping to run off with the little girl's. In order to be effective, the demons' threats must include the name of the person who was cursed, and so for as long as the name Bilqis was not uttered, the child would be protected. In the palace she was referred to as the "little queen" or "the princess," and even when she came to the throne, the name of Bilqis was never heard in the streets of the town.

For a long time the king paid no attention to the troubles afflicting his wife's mind: he knew that she was fragile, and the nurse had informed him of her violent, inexplicable reaction toward their child. But that was women's business! But then her two attempts to set fire to the palace made him realize that it was a genie's evil power that had seized hold of Ishta's mind. The danger was great. The walls of the palace were built of stone and cob and were supported by a hardwood structure that could easily catch fire. The moment he heard the news, the king made an irreversible decision: he would no longer visit his wife, but neither would he deny or cast her aside. Thus, there would be no other children, which meant there would be no son. Any child born of another bed he might have honored would in advance be barred from any rights to kingdom or property. Thus, he imposed his daughter upon the country as his sole successor. When she was born he had hoped she would exercise power in the way women do, through their husbands. He wanted a brilliant son-in-law, as rich and powerful as himself. Then, at the age of four the little girl was designated to be the future queen, the king found that he thought less about marrying her off than of forging her education, so that she might preserve the kingdom and come into her inheritance.

He sheltered the child from her mother. He forbade anyone, especially the child, from entering the quarters set aside for Ishta in the farthest wing of the palace. The king was a man of impulse. He had fallen in love with Ishta the instant he had set her free from the cave, when he saw her birdlike face with her large astonished eyes emerge from the darkness. Once Ishta became a threat to the kingdom, his love for her ceased, it vanished as if it had never existed. Yet, he refused to have the mother of his child put to death. She had committed no murder, no blood law obliged him to spill more blood. But he put her aside and never desired to see her again. This tendency toward swift reversals of feeling and the power his reason could exercise over his feelings had protected him more than once from suffering, and it had made him inflexible, a natural commander. Friends who were guilty of crimes became strangers to him the moment he learned of their wrongdoing. Only the princess, little Bilqis, passed through her childhood without eliciting the king's abrupt reversal of sentiment, his sudden withdrawal of love and trust. Even when the little girl ran off to the forbidden room as if to an impossible refuge, he would have her led back to his quarters without punishing her. In this matter he followed the advice of the tutor he had chosen, a scholar and wise man whom the king would have liked to have had as a teacher himself had he not been preoccupied with ensuring the unity and wealth of the kingdom of Sheba.

From the moment Ishta was locked away, forbidden to go out or to receive visitors, her lamentations could be heard from behind the thick walls of her secret chamber. At the outset, her singing was vigorous, with all the nuances of harmony she had learned as a young woman. Her deep, imploring voice, in a guttural tongue, would bring the song out of a lower register toward higher notes, full of forceful pleading. She added com-

plicated embellishments: *"Boetslala ah ah, tsal, tsala, boitsala..."*
The little girl understood none of it, except that it imparted a
great suffering which seemed to touch her too, even when for
months her entourage barred her from going anywhere near the
chamber where the fire always burned.

Mother!

On this night when she has decided to leave, the queen is
prepared to try everything. She has the consent of the council—
can she not bring her mother closer?

"Mother!"

Ishta makes no attempt to turn around, nor does she
cease her rocking from one foot to the other as she continues
chanting, offering up fragments of lamentations whose melodies
have gradually been broken away, splintered. The song has become a cry, a shrill expression of insurmountable anguish. Bilqis
moves slowly toward the figure by the altar. She stands behind
her, by the armchair; sometimes the woman with the mechanical gestures slumps exhausted into her seat. For the first time
since her childhood, Bilqis dares to touch her mother. She
places a hand on her shoulder and, with a gesture both tender
and firm, sketches a caress. There is no reaction. Her mother's
shoulder rises and falls with the motion of walking in place,
spasmodic.

"Mother!"

The girl puts her arms around the old woman's frail body
and tries to make her turn around. She dares not force her, impose her will or show her authority.

Then she becomes aware of the guard's presence. She had
seen him upon entering the room but paid no attention to the
familiar figure. Now in this hesitant interlude, as she stands lost
and helpless by her mother—who no longer fights her off but
yet does not respond to her pleading—the queen lifts her gaze
toward the man with the dagger in his belt. He is leaning
against his spear, his head covered in a tight scarf, the thick bar
of a mustache across his face: Bilqis looks at him imploringly:

Do something! You stand there watching her all day long, you must know how to reach her, how to get her to react, how to bring her back to me! Move! Help me! But her request remains unsaid, and the guard, whose strict instructions are to respond only if Ishta becomes dangerous, does not move. The ravaged woman, however, is not unaware of her daughter's pleading. The pressure on her shoulder has changed slightly, it is now both gentler and less sure. This woman, who has lost the use of language, is sensitive to everything transmitted through subtle sensation, everything that passes through silence. In Bilqis' hands, Ishta's body begins to rotate, slowly but steadily. She interrupts neither her foot movements nor her chanting, but where rhythm and melody had disappeared, something new has taken their place and is forming. Her steps now keep a rhythm, and while her words remain incomprehensible, fragments of an unknown language, the song now follows a line, it has become continuous. Her voice has grown calmer, it has dropped in timber, she is able once again to modulate. Her twisted broken body, permanently bent, now stands straighter; it finds its center around her backbone, and her left shoulder is once again horizontal with her right.

Bilqis does not move nor does she try to accompany her; she lets the thin body glide between her hands. She can feel the hard bones beneath her mother's clothing. Gradually, the woman's face is revealed: her drawn features, framed by unkempt hair that is matted in unruly locks, her deep wrinkles, her cracked lips, and above all, her eyes set deep in their sockets—empty eyes, drowning as they stare into an invincible pain. The woman before her seems to have preserved nothing human beyond her pain; she has retreated into a distant, foreign world, buried herself in a wilderness without bearings or memory, as if she were in a carapace. To restore this woman to herself and to her past, to a life overburdened with memory, would be an act of violence. If the young queen were to catch her gaze and oblige her to stop, to react and respond and acknowledge the bonds of mother and child, it would be an unbearable confrontation with the truth. To reach out and bring her back from the depths of her monotonous chanting would strip her of her only solace. So Bilqis refrains from acting; she accepts her mother's refusal of a world that has brought too much suffering. Oblivion is her only hope for tranquility. The ravaged woman's body slips away from between her daughter's hands and turns, and Bilquis does nothing to try to stop her or hold her back. Ishta faces the altar; her chanting is once again disjointed, and her steps no longer follow any rhythm.

Tears stream down Bilqis' face, tears of consent, different from those that overcame her at the end of the council: "I agree," she promises, "to refrain from asking more from my mother than what she can give. I shall renounce those forms of tenderness and recognition that she cannot return and grant her the right to dwell in the world where she has found refuge. I understand why my father has never attempted to have her exorcised. The demons protect her from that which she has never been able to see or to accept. I shall grant her the form of love that she needs: I shall leave her in peace. I shall go away, not to forget, but to begin my quest for other horizons, those I might find in the land of the god who stayed the hand of the father—this Yahveh, for whom a human's life is worth more than a ram's. I shall go to meet the king who knows how to unravel enigmas, and I shall answer all the 'whys,' even those that have ravaged my mother's mind."

Chapter six

The sheets rise and fall to the rhythm of the young woman's deep, peaceful breathing; her body quivers still with brief shudders. Each time, the contemplation of a woman after love-making gives Piero a rush of sensations. There is a fleeting moment when acrid odors veil sweeter ones, when her skin absorbs the candlelight and shines with a particular brilliance. Her face opens to reveal her true beauty, devoid of any powders or artifices, and her body describes angles and curves possible only in moments of complete abandonment. The slightest details of her being express plenitude. To be the cause of such splendor and fulfillment, to bring about this blossoming, is an act of creation worth all the paintings in the world. Piero caresses her with his fingertips and the palms of his hands. He feels the excitement of discovery in all the sensitive places in his body, the quivering of the encounter, the accomplishment of pleasure. Love leads him into a rapture not unlike that induced by painting or drawing. It is like the times when he is covering a wall with shapes and colors, sharing his passion with the viewer, leading him into the depths of an interior or a landscape, into a story which raises him above himself and his everyday life.

Despite his impressive size and strength, Piero knows how to soften his body to express tenderness, the tenderness inspired by any woman who arouses his desire. He mingles eagerness and lightness, passion and delicacy. Even in the moments of greatest fervor, something in him seeks out perfection, seeks to organize and compose. He attaches as much importance to the sensations he gives as to those he receives. For Piero, pleasure does not end in the same place as it does for other men.

Once a woman's body has reached a place where he can no longer follow, leaving him only the fascination of the mystery he has provoked, he withdraws gently from his companion's side and puts on a robe. He observes her, her head and limbs spread against the sheets of pastel blue, pale rose, or ivory; although he is no way involved in the housekeeping in his home, he took the time to choose the fabrics to decorate this room and to have them cut in his father's workshop. Seated on a chair at the foot of the bed, he forces himself to remain still and simply to observe for a time, which always seems so long: a mark of respect, he concludes, for the woman and her pleasure. Then he reaches up to a shelf on the nearest wall for a sheet of paper, a charcoal or a pencil, and a piece of cardboard as a support. He hastily captures the fold of an elbow, the curve of a shoulder, the full and rested flesh of a cheek. He covers her breast with a corner of the sheet to observe the effect beneath the light veil of cloth.

Sandra is a perfect model. She offers her body to him and in exchange, expects nothing more than an equally generous honorarium. Yet there is more than mere mutual accommodation between them. He appreciates the delicacy of her manners, which sets her apart from the girls who ordinarily work as artists' models, and from those fussy country girls who make a show of refusing and then end up surrendering in an excess of graceless debauchery. For over five years he has met with Sandra whenever he is in Borgo, receiving her in this attic room, his private domain above the large studio he has set up in one of his father's old warehouses.

When work is at its most intense, fifteen apprentices and assistants occupy the ground floor to finish figures, enlarge drawings, and copy them onto cartoons before they leave for the church. They then accompany Piero in the exhilarating process of transferring the work to the walls. It is a time of agitation and exaltation, climbing up and down the scaffolding, covering the sometimes rough surfaces with a coating, and blowing pigment through the holes pierced in the cartoons until at last the design is unveiled, often to reveal unexpected qualities or imperfections. It is never possible to predict what will happen. In such moments of fervor, Piero casts off all fear and restraint: He is filled with the exalting sensation of having total mastery over his space. He has the power to bring to life perfect beauty, as well as harmony and depth, the strength of joy, of suffering, and of woe. He instills a reign of silence. The very intensity of their inner quest illuminates the faces of his figures and dismisses pretence, futile agitation, and evil rumors. He invents technical solutions, displays his ingeniousness and the breadth of his imagination; he projects vision. Piero takes all points of view into account: that of the viewer on the ground or in the center of the chapel and that of the painter suspended between earth and sky on his scaffold opposite the frescoes, forgetful of the very existence of a world outside the unique relation between this place, this support, and the subject of the work celebrating the grandeur of God. On his scaffold he thinks, he turns this way and that; with a brushstroke he imposes his ascendancy over the matter that resists him; he caresses, he modifies, he delays, or, on the contrary, acts quickly and directly upon the moist substance; he is borne upon a relentless energy that enlivens him in Sandra's presence and, in an utterly different way, when he is with Silvia, leaving him equally exhausted, unsatisfied but content.

Love-making with Sandra procures moments of great freedom, the opposite of the restraint and modesty that Silvia sometimes displays when they are alone together. His wife constantly hesitates between an instinct for delight, which enables her to take full advantage of the joys of life, and a fear of transgressing, of offending her God, of denying the precepts of Saint

Francis. Was the saint not stubbornly opposed to the demands of his body, which he referred to as "brother ass"? It was the contrast between these two temperaments that Piero found so appealing and which attracted him so irresistibly from the moment he set eyes on her. He saw first a woman who was constantly attentive, ready to act and to decide like an indefatigable watchman, serious and faithful; then he discovered with rapture the young woman who was terrified by her own boldness. "Where does your father live, that I might ask him for your hand?" Despite its incongruity, these were the only words he could utter when he spoke to her for the first time outside the chapel of Santa Maria della Momentana in Monterchi.

Sandra sleeps stretched out across the bed while Piero sits by her side. On the paper his pencil caresses the harmonious curve of her shoulder; he never takes his eyes from her, in order to reproduce her contours with precision, and yet it is another shoulder that dominates his memory—less full, more fragile, a shoulder he glimpsed at the edge of a fountain on a merry morning in spring, nearly ten years ago now. It is not the first time that Sandra's presence has led him back to Silvia, that all the words withheld and restrained when he is with his wife come tranquilly to mind after his love-making with Sandra. The need to speak out is transformed into a silent dialogue that he will try to resume when he is at home.

He puts the drawing he has begun to the side, for now a new idea has taken hold: a story, one he knows well because he has lived it, which is to be told in a rapid succession of pictures scribbled on paper like so many sketches for the lower section of an altar painting. He takes a large sheet of paper, cuts it into rectangles, and on each one outlines an image that follows the thread of a story as it unfolds in silence. For once his drawing does not praise God through the saints, so marvelously distant, but through the example of an ordinary existence with which he is intimately acquainted: moments of simple happiness experienced by an unexceptional man. Are these not more exalting, more fitting to honor the presence of God at the heart of life, than the grand exploits of beings too perfect to seem accessible?

"I was on my way back from Florence after a long stay in Perugia," he murmurs. "Domenico's betrayal had devastated me. He chose another associate for his new commission. I knew that such a moment would come, that we could not be bound together for our entire life, that one day I would have to become my own master, that my turn would come to besiege the princes and patrons on my own. But I did not feel ready for this other profession, where chance plays as great a role as the ability to negotiate. I did not consider myself capable of going to the court Domenico had suggested to me and charming the prince, who was looking for young painters to introduce new art forms at his estate. I dreaded setting out. The entire country was in confusion after the upheaval in the council and the turbulent visit of Byzantine nobles. Our little northern towns had a new master; we had been sold by the pope to Florence to cover the expenses of the council. The notables were restless. My father used the opportunity to cement his alliances, raise prices, and secure contracts. I could no longer stand all this turmoil, this sort of internal war replacing the military war, which had only just come to an end.

"My mother suggested I go to Monterchi, to get some rest at her family home. As a child, I had always enjoyed our visits to the farm. I would test my ever growing strength by lifting the hay and goading the sluggish beasts; I would run along the paths and disappear for hours with the peasant children whom I already treated like my assistants. I had also been in charge of building a real cabin—with a stonework structure and a vault made of boughs—on the slopes of the Citerna. It was in this place that I experienced my first moments of despair and, paradoxically, it was here as well that I discovered the strength of determination, which would shape the course of my life. One day when I was trying to carve a tree trunk with a decorative shape I had carefully planned in a drawing, I accidentally gouged my hand. The cut was very deep. I thought I would lose the use of my fingers. In that moment I realized I could not live if I could not draw, if I could not order space, imagine interiors, grind colors, or design shapes and faces. Young Marta, our servant who had gifts of healing, worked marvels—she treated my wound with unguents and concoctions, incantations and entreaties. The accident took place there, by the side of the fountain outside the chapel of Santa Maria della Momentanta. As soon as I was better, I returned to Borgo and asked my father to find me an apprenticeship. I went from studio to studio, from one town to the next, depending on the commissions I was working on, and I never returned to Monterchi."

Sandra turns on the bed, letting out a long sigh. She lifts her left arm straight up then places it next to her ear, hiding her shoulder. As she stretches, she reveals a breast, its nipple erect as if asking or demanding something of him. Piero is tempted to interrupt what he is doing and return to Sandra. He is tempted to put down his pencil to reach out and resume his caresses, to draw her plump round breast in another way. But just as his arm begins to move, the fragile tip of her breast softens; it is as if he is pulled inside it. The areola around him opens out, becomes smooth and wide as it spreads outward. The artist's hand returns to the paper, to a sketch evoking another woman, in another time and another place. He resumes his silent soliloquy and pays no more attention to Sandra, who drifts in her inner world.

"The moment I arrived in Monterchi, I wanted to see my cabin in the forest. What would I find after so many years? I found it both astonishingly intact and completely destroyed. A shepherd had used it as a shelter; he had maintained it, but had also strengthened it and shored it up. Boards now covered the openings of the main room. The long corridor of boughs leading into the main room had been opened out.—the balance of shadow and light that I had created was completely destroyed. I had conceived the room as a well of light surrounded by shadow. The moment you stepped into the cabin's dark entrance, your eye would be drawn by the light coming from the main room, beyond the dark passageway. The light filtered through the trees and onto a wide clearing. I had wanted to create an opening in the shape of an oculus, although my apprentice masons had been clumsy and had not managed to round the angular edges.

"But what was most important to me was still there: Deep in the darkness, protected by the thick forest, was the place where fine luminous rays of light penetrated the canopy of branches and leaves. I had captured and directed them so that they would become light sources, one from the east, the other from the west. Thus from sunrise to sunset the main room was filled with light of varying intensities depending upon the time of day or the season; it was never a harsh light, somehow it always seemed to interplay with the shapes and shadows it formed without crushing them. The leaves created a dappled light, iridescent with dewdrops, a light of endless play and variations. The room seemed a perfect workplace to produce the drawings I had begun to accumulate and for my passion, which was growing with each passing day: I had gone there twice, until I had the accident that nearly left me a cripple and deprived me the use of my right hand.

"Thus, when I happened upon this very place where I had made my first creations, it was not so much the pile of manure at the threshold that troubled me, nor its pervasive smell, nor the accumulation of now nameless colorless things in the room I had designated for my work: I was devastated by the destruction of the light! The shepherd had neither seen it, nor felt it; I had not known how to communicate my feelings through the design of the cabin. It was clear that I had not known how to make the light an absolute necessity, or its beauty an indispensable presence. The lack of any aesthetic awareness on the part of the man who had mutilated my cabin was like a personal failure to me. For after all, we both belonged to the same human race; I felt a solidarity with him. Still, I was affected by his lack of taste, his complete imperviousness to the language of nature, his inability to decipher it and make it his own. Until that moment I had condemned the opinion of certain humanists who held that beauty was the exclusive preserve of an elite—yet this man had proved them right, most brutally! Could it be that for the majority of humans, stupidity and not just ignorance, as well as fear and the search for material comfort had crushed all ability to feel? Or was I the one who had erred by following these humanists, by questioning the behavior of Umbrian shepherds to whom I, in fact, belonged by virtue of my own origins? Had I set off down the wrong path in trying to link my fortune to artists like Domenico who, ultimately, rejected me? I was filled with agony at the thought of everything that separated me from those to whom I was merely trying to offer beauty. What seemed so obvious to me—the pure sensation I had felt when I looked at the light created by multiple refraction—was not something that could be experienced by the very people for whom the frescoes of our churches were intended! Were they the ones lacking some part of their humanity, or was it I who was lost in idle speculation foreign to ordinary human beings? Should I perhaps return to a more ordinary, everyday life, give up my wild dreams, and rediscover the simplicity of humdrum occupations? Should I create a shelter from the storm, tend to the manure, produce heat, and ensure the bare minimum for my subsistence, in the simple celebration of God's glory?

"On my way home I stopped off at Santa Maria della Momentana. The door was wide open, which was rare except when mass was being celebrated by the priest, who was rather aloof and often absent. This little church with its low, rounded vaults was reserved for discreet and private worship. My grandmother attributed the healing of my hand to the prayers she had offered at the feet of the Virgin therein. I had often had occasion to witness her religious fervor; I would stand back in a posture of silent contemplation, the only posture that comes naturally to me in a holy place. I do not take an active role in religious ceremonies, something holds me back. I cannot perform the meticulous gestures and rituals. I feel that I am celebrating God and am in his service, but I bear in mind the most varied and contradictory aspects of his creation. My painting renders thanks to him for my existence in the world, and I seek to raise beauty and harmony to the highest degree. Yet all the while I am aware that death, suffering, and ugliness are an ever-present and constant threat. I was incapable of sharing my grandmother's simple fervor, but I did join her in prayer in an active way, by making a wish: if I could regain the use of my hand, and if I became an artist, I would replace the fresco of the Virgin above the altar with a real painting! Upon each of my visits I had been dismayed by the picture's dullness and the imprecision of the pale and clumsy contours of this gilt-crushed figure meant to represent the mother of God.

"When I went into the little church again after fifteen years of apprenticeship and painting, the fresco seemed even more unbearable to me. How could a painter have so scorned the Virgin and his own self to the point of afflicting Mary with a face whose eyes were devoid of any expression and whose mouth wore a bitter sneer? How could he have placed next to her such an ugly child, surrounded by two angels who seemed anxious to flee? I stood by the door in the shadow as I always do in churches that do not belong to me, where I am not the master of their transformation or their décor.

"There was a woman moving about the church, carrying out her duties, and she seemed quite ordinary to me at first, a housekeeper with her twig broom and a gray rag, her hair protected by a kerchief that was as drab as her clothing. She was moving the benches and the statues in order to dust. But I was wrong—there was nothing mechanical or ungainly about her gestures. She was working with order and efficiency, from left to right, without lingering or exasperation, or even the heavy weariness that comes with habit. She carried out her simple duties with assurance and, visibly, kept to a concerted plan. The succession of her movements was precise; they followed solid curves or lines according to a regular rhythm. She finished by cleaning the altar: When she went up the steps, she stood straight and did not bend over in exaggerated respect. She moved the objects aside more slowly, and preceded each of her gestures with a brief moment of contemplation, without ostentation, without genuflecting as she went by the tabernacle, and without the mechanical bow to which gestures meant to be deferential are so often reduced. She came down from the altar, which was lit by a shaft of light from the round window above the door, the same door where I stood hiding. The vision I had was comprised of two successive images. I merged the sinister, almost grimacing face of the Virgin as it had been painted on the fresco with that of the young girl's rather long face, with her rosy peasant cheeks, her blue eyes, clear and grave—a gaze where a light solemnity was emphasized by the unmistakably noble bearing of her head. The contrast was astonishing. Her throat emerged from an unusual square neckline, from the layers of clothing protecting her, and the blue fabric enhanced the freshness of her skin.

"She was about to leave—I hid, I wanted to go on watching her without being seen. Something about this young woman disturbed me: she seemed rooted in the most ordinary material dimension of things, and yet she clearly respected the harmony of this holy place, and sought to give a certain form of beauty to the succession of her gestures.

"Quite suddenly she went out the door and was transformed by the sun and the soft April air. With a quick gesture she removed the cloth covering her head and freed her curls, then with a light step, she ran to the fountain. All grace and smiles, she dipped her hands into the water, lifted her widespread fingers to splash her face, and lowered her delicate lips to her cupped palms to drink. Giggling, she splashed her face, then unfastened her outer garment. Beneath it was a lightweight shift. She loosened the neck until her shoulder was bared—a frail, delicate, slightly rounded shoulder, not yet a woman's. She stroked it with her damp fingers, while the sun caused the drops of water to glisten against her pale skin, the faintest pink. From a distance I could imagine its velvet texture. Then she quickly closed her shift and lifted the protective outer garment back onto her shoulders.

"I left the rear of the church where I had been hiding and walked along the path as if I were coming directly from the forest. When she became aware of my presence, she blushed: She was no fool! She knew I had happened upon her in her semi-nudity. She did not respond to me with outrage or provocation, but with a discreet modesty, neither offended nor guilty, which was all the more touching for the fact that in the church she had been acting with authority, as if she were mistress of the place. She met my gaze calmly and did not move back. I stepped forward. Her greeting was cordial but reserved, addressed not to me, but to the heavens whose protection she invoked. That gave a sacred dimension to the moment, placed our meeting under the sign of those elements essential to life:

'All praise be yours, my Lord, through Sister Water
So useful, lowly, precious, and pure.'

"She was quoting the *Canticle to the Sun,* by Saint Francis of Assisi, not as if it were some propitiatory formula recited by rote, but as if the words had been carefully chosen, as if they were a part of herself that she was offering to me, revealing her identity. She joined two parts of the world that had seemed irreconcilable to me: she knew what beauty was, she recognized it as indispensable to life, and yet she was still similar to the shepherd who had occupied my cabin; nothing in her attitude excluded or rejected the world of simple people to which she, too, belonged.

I was deeply troubled: This was the woman who could give unity to my life, who could bring together both everyday demands and those of my art, the dimension of the family and the artist's wanderings. An extraordinary strength I did not know I had suddenly urged me to say: "Where does your father live that I might ask him for your hand?"

"'I do not know if my father has already been called to heaven or if he still has a dwelling on the earth,' she replied, responding to my question with simplicity and an utterly natural manner. 'Since God has placed you upon my path, I shall be willing to meet you in other circumstances, to see if what he intends for us is quite what you imagine.'

"The way she phrased her answer was doubly pleasing: my manner had not frightened her, and she had surely read enough books to have acquired a feeling and a taste for language.

"Her unknown origins were not an obstacle to our marriage. My grandmother had long appreciated the young girl to whom the priest of her favorite church had entrusted his domain. She was surrounded by an aura of mystery, but the piety of her world was reassuring. The Franciscans had given her as a baby to the woman who tended their garden of medicinal plants. They continued to supervise her education, and she learned from them far more than what was necessary for a young country girl. Silvia had never asked to know more: neither where she came from nor the reasons for the Franciscan community's concern. She did not want to know. Something held her back at the threshold to truth; an instinct protected her— protected *us*, she would say on the rare occasions when, once we were married, we touched on the subject."

Absorbed by his story, illustrating it as the words formed in his mind, Piero did not hear Sandra move. She slid toward him with a movement of her upper body, then leaned on her elbow to look at his drawing: "Where is that fountain? And that strange statue? They have nothing to do with me! What is the point of me lying here without moving, giving you this pose and that, if you are not even looking at me! What a strange landscape. I cannot even tell where it is!"

Even Piero finds it hard to recognize the place. What has he been drawing while his mind has been reconstructing the past, putting it together with words and phrases? What did the sculpture adorning the fountain in Monterchi really look like? He cannot recall it with precision; his memory fails him. He will have to go back there at the first opportunity to verify how the stone embellishment has been put together. But was his drawing not actually an attempt to draw another fountain? Did he not set off on Silvia's trail only to find himself transported to the little courtyard of the Queen of Sheba, in the presence of the hoopoe and the tree with its flaming red flowers beneath the dazzling sun of the East?

Sandra sits up with a sudden movement of vexation. Piero is no longer looking at her; he does not even reply to her questions. Sandra, Silvia, the queen…How uselessly complicated his life suddenly seems to him. And still there is nothing with which to pay back the debt he owes to his father, beyond achieving success and the consolidation of the family fortune. Not one of his women has provided him with an heir— his offspring could have even been arranged through Sandra, with the help of skillfully worded legal documents and Silvia's tacit consent.

He stands up. On the other side of the bed, the young woman is getting dressed. She is much younger than Silvia, and yet she has already lost any trace of childhood. In this moment, nothing is required of her. Still, she continues to strike a pose, as she does for every circumstance in life. Suddenly a question comes to mind, one which Piero must ask as unexpectedly as his abrupt proposal to Silvia by the fountain in Monterchi. He must know, before Sandra disappears from this room and from his existence: "Have you ever been with child from me?"

The irony of her reply startles him: "There's no risk of that, as you well know! I did not want to believe the rumors I had heard from the other girls when I first came to your studio. But they were right. The fine ladies of Borgo may blame your wife because it suits them to do so, but we know otherwise! And from experience. This is not a reproach; it's quite practical. One less worry, one major worry."

Silvia is still at her writing desk. She continues her task, taking no heed of the passing hours, of the house bustling with life around her and without her. She has been completely absorbed and is so distracted in her replies to the servants' questions, that in the end they have stopped asking anything of her. She is convinced that her writing is not for the sake of the words themselves but for the power they have to lead toward art. She is fulfilling the mission with that God has invested her: to save Piero from the attraction that Rome—that diabolical city—exerts upon him. She began to compose this text at Fra Bartolomeo's behest, she has continued because she likes it and enjoys it, and sees no fault or sin in what she is doing. She feels content in the shadow of the house. Thanks to her husband's understanding and her mother-in-law's indulgence, she has organized her life in the way that is most conducive to her: removed from others and from perpetual immersion in conversation and noise. She has no more desire to emerge from her seclusion thanshe had to leave the garden at Monterchi in the old days.

Piero often talks to her of the humanist writers who cross his path. Full of their own knowledge and the social class they represent, preoccupied by trivial incidents, they are scornful of him. There is little difference between the petty drama of their lives and the perpetual scheming of the household Silvia is in charge of. Last week two maidservants quarreled because Silvia had complimented one of them on a task, while the other claimed she had done most of it. Mario, the chamberlain, fears the power of the cook, Marta, and of late has not been hesitant inconcealing any culinary misdemeanors so that Marta will have to shoulder the blame once it is too late to do anything about it. Yesterday on his way out, a visitor gave the servant who handed him his hat a gratuity that was greater than the one he had given the porter on a previous visit, so the porter devised a way to have the new servant dismissed on a false pretext. Silvia is constantly called upon to investigate, to weigh the arguments, and to pass judgment on the sort of trifles which only human stupidity attaches importance, but which it is impossible to ignore. Individuals identify themselves with such trivial preoccupations and feel scorned if their mistress does not take their worries to heart. She has read as much in her books, and has the proof of it every day.

Raised in Monterchi, in the garden of the woman who grew the medicinal plants, Silvia used to belong to the world of ordinary people, yet remained persuaded that her origins linked her to another milieu. In her heart of hearts she believed that people everywhere were the same, at the mercy of their own insignificance, whatever their greatness might be. She felt close to the theory developed in the books by Alberti that Piero brought to her: the individual must become aware of himself, of his singularity, and display it openly to others so that he might better appreciate it and accomplish his role as guide, after God, of the universe. She had considerable admiration for Alberti, as much for the philosopher as for the architect. She admired his powers of invention and creation, but was also aware of his burning ambition and the scorn he reserved for those who were neither useful nor necessary. Piero would have liked to have known him better, to further the debate on perspective, but the master persisted in avoiding the son of the merchant from Borgo. Piero had rushed to Urbino to see him, but Alberti, with supreme nonchalance, left the town without warning only moments before they were to meet.

If Silvia prefers to remain in the shadows, it is a personal choice: before she even knew the word humility she practiced the virtue while deepening her knowledge of the teachings of Saint Francis. It was no effort for her to follow Fra Bartolomeo's advice. She hides deep within Piero's house, convinced she will find nothing greater outside than what she already possesses within her home. Her preference for solitude also enables her to avoid the question she reads on every face: why have they not been given a child? A thousand explanations and a thousand words of advice have been offered by the maidservants or by the fine ladies of the town. She knows what people are saying, she has heard the rumors that the most petty among them delight in relaying. She has heard anything and everything: that her obscure origins will have negative consequences for those who will come after her; that Piero gives elsewhere that which she cannot keep for herself; that she locks her husband up and so he rebels against this additional constraint; that she is sheltering a witch under her roof—Marta, the cook from Monterchi, who knows how to speak to the wolves when they threaten the village and who stirs mysterious potions on her fire; that out of pride she has refused the services offered by well-meaning and influential women to help her in her distress; that she has been reading too many books, and this is unnatural for a woman;and for all these reasons, she has been deprived of the conjugal fruits. It is also rumored that she goes alone to church, where she displays a suspicious devotion to the Virgin and Saint Francis.

Silvia herself does not think she has been cursed by God, but the fact that he has withheld the blessing he grants to all women is a source of despair for her. And over time her courage has been eroded: she no longer dares to meet the gaze of the women openly direct their gaze at her empty belly. The text that she has been writing with Fra Bartolomeo's help allows her to feel that she is at last carrying something inside her, something she can share with Piero; the void, the absence of a child, seems to weigh less.

"Signora, Rosita is dead!"

She had not heard the maidservant come in, but now she is shocked at the fateful words. Death in her house! Death constantly circling her, around all humankind, from birth. Even Saint Francis could not persuade her to see death as a deliverance. She loves life, loves to feel Piero's body against hers, to see the flowers in the field in summer, the fire in the hearth when it is freezing outside; she loves Marta's juniper pies, and she does not want to leave this world before seeing the child, her child, their child... "Dear God," she pleads, raising her eyes toward the crucifix fastened to the right-hand corner of her writing desk. "Dear God, do not abandon us!"

The winter night has fallen, deep, damp and cold. Piero's heavy step resounds on the tiled floor. An unusual silence weighs upon the house. The moment he pushed the door open, Mario motioned to him: they are waiting for him in the dining room.

"One of the kitchenmaids has died," Silvia tells him before he has even crossed the room, "and her body has just been taken away to be burned. They have started the bonfires again at the gates to the city. The plague has come back, right to our house. We have to leave quickly, before anyone else falls ill. Marta has already gone ahead to prepare our refuge in Monterchi. We will be staying at your mother's home. Oh, if only the garden of medicinal herbshad not been left untended. If only my dear little mother were still alive—she got along so well with Marta and shared her talents with her. We have so little time, Piero, we must leave tomorrow!"

Silvia stands shivering next to the fireplace, where the fire is crackling. For once, she is not holding a book. Her features are drawn; she is worried, distressed, overwhelmed, and Piero has no answer to give her for her fear of death or her incapacity to give a new life. "It's your fault," Sandra had flung back at him. It is he who is guilty, and he cannot confess this to Silvia because he would have to talk about Sandra. Silvia knows—of course she does, the town is too small to hide such things—but as long as this affair does not cross the threshold of their home and, above all, as long as no words are spoken, it will remain without significance. Piero walks across the large room toward Silvia and folds her into his arms; he squeezes her, pressing her into him and resting his chin at the place where a thin cloth is clipped to cover her hair. "Forgive me, forgive me," he murmurs, so quietly she cannot hear him. She shifts in his arms, he is afraid of stifling her. "Forgive me," he says again.

"Forgive you? For what? You do not want to leave?" And she stands straight, abruptly, her face full of fear.

"Do not worry," he continues, drawing her head to his chest. "I'll gather up my drawings. We shall continue the story of the queen, Bilqis, since that is her name."

Bilqis—the queen! Even at such a time Piero cannot stop thinking about his painting.

Chapter seven

The queen gradually succumbs to the rhythm of the journey. How long have they been gone? How far have they come from the first obstacle they crossed, the mountains to the north of Sheba? The dangerous and exhausting passage over the steep mountain passes, the terrifying yet marvelous sight of each precipice, and the slow meandering through thick fog have become mere memories, like the mosaic formed against the slopes by the irrigated fields, the patches of green enlivening the brown. They encountered the noisy joviality of local inhabitants, who would warn each other of a caravan's arrival by calling from mountaintop to mountaintop. When a caravan drew near the path defended by their village, they would hurtle down the steep slopes and accompany the long column with song and their calls for as long as the caravan was on their territory. This warm welcome was also a way to keep watch. Ready to intervene, armed men stood guard on the rooftops of houses whose brown stone had faded into the rock of the mountaintops. As soon as the border of the village had been crossed, they would withdraw, to be immediately replaced by their neighbors a hundred away, who had already been informed.

That harsh, green, and rocky country—the border between two areas of desert—is far behind them. Their days are now like those on the stony, dusty plateaus, grayish despite the sun. The rare inhabitants lay low, hiding or passing by far off in the distance, perched proudly on skeleton-thin camels. Nothing matters anymore but the road andthe slow and continuous progression from sunrise to sunset, the constant jostlingthat is hard on one's back despite the cushions, the throats parched by dust, despite the water with its traces of iron that is drunk straight from goatskins -- one's innards twisting with all kinds of ill-defined aches. Even the goal seems to recede, Jerusalem vanishes into a dream belonging to another life. Desires are annihilated, melt into a waiting that has become the purpose of everything: how far to the next stage, or until the causes of discomfort are relieved, even temporarily; how far until the next significant event that will quell the boredom of long hours spent with one's legs folded in the narrow space of the palanquin. Everything seems futile, made weary by the contemplation of an unchanging landscape. The caravan rolls along the edge of the desert: the beasts laden with heavy packsaddles can move more easily along hard stony ground than in the sand, where they sink in. The continuous ascent and descent seems endless. From time to time the majestic vastness of the dunes, with their harmonious movement and color changing from pale to copper hues, can be glimpsed in the distance. Farther to the north they will spend long days crossing the sands, perhaps even weeks; they will lose count. In the morning, when the caravan leader's call rings out, the queen's concerns are nothing more than material details, both mundane and essential: the quantity of water she can use, which varies according to the distance from one well to the next; the mood of the mules carrying her palanquin, the milk supply of the camels. She has not abandoned the prerogatives and preoccupations of a queen, but circumstances have relieved her from her regular responsibilities. The only news from Sheba comes with rare messengers. And in order for the voyage to proceed with ease through this hostile and foreign territory, she has delegated her powers. Nothing depends on her, neither the route nor the daily decisions regarding the organization of her retinue, which consists of a few rare women—to serve the queen—and a chaotic crowd of men who are essential for the grooming and care of the camels, supervising their merchandise, and for the safety of their everyday life.

She chose their leader, a short little man, dry and heavy-set, with a stiff and prominent mustache, who is quick but sparing with his words. He had arrived in Sheba late in childhood; he belongs to one of the influential tribes of the region, and he knows their customs, their concerns, and how to negotiate and deal with them tactfully in order to prevent raids. The caravan is transporting so many treasures that it could easily be the target of envy and attack. This man knows how to lead the camel drivers and the guides without wounding their pride, as any failure to respect their customs would be a serious and irreparable error. He gives them their just reward, taking into consideration not only their love of money but their susceptibilities; while accepting of their gestures of generosity, he ensures that the queen and her retinue will be in no way obliged to them for anything or dependent on them in any way. He puts their endurance, their courage, and their immense patience in the midst of the harsh elements to good use, while never forgetting their unpredictability—freedom is their most precious possession. At times he must resort to violence to punish one of them, and he remains indifferent to their suffering or even death, for he attaches no more value to life than they do. Thus he commands respect and obedience, but to the queen he is terrifying. Holding tight to the handles of her palanquin, she is struggling with herself not to rise and remind him of his rank, or to demand a more lenient sentence, the effects of which would be disastrous: she would compromise the ever fragile authority the caravan leader exerts over the nomads. He manages to maintain an equilibrium between the men of the desert and the guards from Sheba, sedentary men who have changed greatly with the habits of the town. He has a way of helping them get along together, and while he cannot prevent the occasional altercation, he ensures that their strength is pooled for the common good.

On more than one occasion they have had to take up arms to respond to attacks or threats of intimidation. A troop of warriors came at them on their galloping camels and surrounded the camp; yet the queen was not frightened, and this time she felt neither the disgust nor the despondency of the battle where her father was killed. In this nomadic existence, life and death take on another meaning, and the gulf between them becomes more tenuous, and the relations among people are changed. This is something the queen experiences every day. She is not privy to secrets and agrees to remain silent and passive in this milieu, where life, most often, means little more than survival. Removed from consequences and events, she seeks only to protect herself. There is nothing to do but wait, to endure with constancy and patience the physical discomfort, unpleasantness, and sometimes even pain imposed upon her fragile body. She must also overcome the irritation brought on by the mannerisms of this man she has chosen to lead the expedition—he is all the better adapted to his duties precisely because he is different from her and is insensitive to everything that matters to her. She spends her time with Nour at insignificant tasks, the only ones they have room for behind the stifling curtains of the palanquin: beauty care, frequently inspecting her appearance—futile things which, at the palace, were relaxing, a childhood pleasure, but that are now vital to deflect the constant aggression of the elements—the dry winds, the stifling heat, the invasion of dust and sand—and to maintain her dignity as a woman. She will worry later about forging her destiny; for now she plans to put this leisure time to good use by deciphering some of the tablets Nour has collected on the civilization of Jerusalem, about Solomon and his father, David, about their holy book and their god, Yahweh. But in the canopy-draped palanquin, constantly rocked by sudden and unpredictable movements, crushed by heat and tossed by the wind, any task that demands attention and precision is out of the question. When at last the long-awaited evening pause arrives, the queen has only one urgent desire: to withdraw into her tent, lie down on ground that is absolutely still, and try to forget that most of the day she has been a bag of bones shaken in every direction. All she wants is to escape the nauseating smell of the palanquin, which incense and lavish doses of perfume can do nothing to dissipate. This evening the caravan leader has announced that the queen will not sleep in the little two-sided tent, which is quick to set up, as she usually does.She will lodge in the ceremonial tent, with its circular wooden frame covered with several thicknesses of ram's hide and a richly embroidered curtain that opens down the middle to be held open on either side by fine ropes braided with gold. This is where the queen receives the tribal chiefs she must honor and impress: they will now be passing through regions where the inhabitants are known to be particularly rebellious and threatening. Only Bakhit's mediation will allow them to go as far as Aqaba without having to pay an exorbitant tribute, so they will camp here for several days in the hopes of luring Bahkit to the tent and of convincing him, with choice gifts, to protect them on their way.

The queen now has to wait for the heavy tent to be set up and for the turmoil caused by the sudden change in their routine to subside, while the inhabitants of this vast town that springs up at every caravan stop find their places for the night. She had stepped down out of her palanquin a little while before, whereas the end of the column has not yet reached the entry to the camp. The queen refuses to shut herself away in the temporary shelter that has been erected; it is too narrow and confined. She stays outdoors, wrapped in her veils to shield her from the relentless heat of the sun. Clouds of dust rise as the beasts of burden are unloaded: to be relieved of their loads, the camels must be made to kneel, but they grow stubborn and irritated by the proximity of water. Men and beasts jostle together and cry out. No one is safe if one of the powerful animals suddenly attempts to break away. The camels seem to be laughing, making fun, as they move their muzzles back and forth: "Ah-hah! You want me to obey you—let's have some fun first!"

The queen takes a few awkward steps to test her limbs. Her body responds: She can move, raise her arms, turn her head in either direction. The pleasure she feels is out of proportion with the simplicity of her gestures. Nour has just joined her; she stands by her side in silence. The silence between them restores peace to her body; it is a blessing after a day spent together in the palanquin, obliged to make conversation in an attempt to escape one's obsession with heat, thirst, and the brutal rocking. Evening is falling, it is still very hot, but something in the air heralds the nocturnal change in temperature. There is a bustle of activity nearby, around the tents and the braying camels. The two women cannot hear a thing, only the evening wind whistling quietly in their ears. Grains of sand sting their skin, and in the morning they will try to smooth away the irritating consequences with thick unguents. But they do not hurry away to protect themselves, because they are captivated by the beauty and magic of the place—a magic to which the busy men around them remain insensitive, absorbed as they are by what is useful, by water supplies and cattle feed.

The splendor of their surroundings did not strike the queen and her entourage at once, but came over them gradually. At first their gaze was dazzled by the strength of the sun when they tried to look outside the palanquin, and blunted by the monotony of too many stony plateaus. They had to take time to learn to see again. They sought out the shadow of the palm trees planted by the edge of the well where the caravan stopped. They walked forward slowly, mindful of where they put their feet, covered only in the cloth-soled slippers they wore inside the palanquin to protect the carpets and cushions. They did not lift their eyes from the reddish, rocky earth, where rare bushes had sprouted during the last rain many moons ago. No sooner unsaddled, the camels rushed to find this cloud-given food: in keeping with the tradition among the desert men, the dromedaries would be allowed to roam free all night long; they knew better than any other creature how to find the hidden tufts vital to their survival.

The two women watched the camels as they set off, then, raising their heads, they were caught unaware, captivated by the landscape. Rocky peaks, veering from ochre to pink then red to mauve beneath the setting sun, stood proudly reaching for the sky like slender curving sculptures, tracing a dance of lines and shapes, drawing rhythms and cadences as they formed a protective barrier all around the circular valley in which the wadi they were following took its source. To the north, the peaks opened out onto a sea of dunes whose gentle curves leaned in unison toward the east, with harmonious scrolls and astonishing variations in color. From one spot to the next, from the summit of the dune to the edge of the folds that shaped it, the colors would shift from copper to a soft cream, silver would blend into to gold, alabaster turned into a dark resin, and shadow overcame brilliance. In the low-angled light the shape of the dunes stood out clearly, forming a movement that seemed to carry on for eternity.

The queen feels drawn, as if she cannot resist this world into which they will enter as soon as Bakhit offers them his protection. She sees this universe as her own origin, the land of her leaving and her arriving, the only one which might possibly meet all her expectations.

As a child she often saw the desert at the gates to her city. Her father isolated her from this hostile environment—the home of the most rebellious tribes, a realm of aridity, impossible to tame, stubbornly resistant to irrigation, to the construction of dams and the development of verdant villages. Despite the harsh conditions prevalent in these lands—the implacable harshness, the terrifying emptiness, the destructive heat of day and bitter cold of the star-filled nights—the little queen ha always felt compelled to discover the desert for herself. She was filled with happiness the day hertutor gave voice and substance her longing: he spoke to her of the desert as a place of ultimate quest, of profound contemplation, as a place where man might at last attain complete harmony with himself, and be closest to the truth of the universe.

The queen gazes toward the northern pass, following her thoughts, and unaware of the stranger approaching the camp. At first she thinks he is a part of the landscape, a form made of sand, driven by the wind from beyond the edge of the desert to the stony amphitheater where the well is situated – the place where all living things converge. Then the almost circular shape stands out against its surroundings because it is moving, progressing in three stages: a straight line to begin with, projected forward in an abrupt motion—it sinks into the ground, serving as a pivotal point for the greater mass following in its wake, which then moves forward in turn with two consecutive steps, first to the right, then the left. Despite the obvious effort involved, the figure is moving quite rapidly. The weight he places upon the cane is a sign of the man's age and fatigue; his body bent, completely folded over upon himself, and supported by his sturdy stick. When he is within earshot of the camp, he raises his head slightly; a faded cloth turban almost completely covers his head. Between the folds of cloth the queen can distinguish his burnished features, his wrinkled copper skin, and his eyes of an extraordinarily light brown.

Two guards rush toward the man with their spears at the ready, while another runs to his side and takes hold of him with such force that the old man collapses. Nour hurries over, and with a vigorous gesture she brushes aside the soldiers who are looking in every which direction for an order or instruction.

"He's one of the survivors of the land of Qoum,. I can tell from his turban and the way he fastens his belt," says the caravan leader, more concerned with how the tents are to be arranged for the visit than with a visitor representing no one but himself. "Leave him alone! He's harmless. For decades that tribe has been steadily losing whatever power it once had. Let the women look after him, that's all he deserves."

The queen has been standing to one side, underneath the palm tree; she shivers Fortunately, his comment was not directed at her, yet she feels it is time for this journey to be over and for this caravan leader to be put in his place, time for him to be reminded that it is a woman who governs his country, a queen. She begins to walk toward the old man, but she stumbles as she takes her first step; she does not have the proper shoes for walking. How has Nour been able to run forward with such agility, without falling? She constantly reveals new and unexpected abilities.

Nour helps the old man to rise and leads him toward the queen. "Great queen pledged unto eternity, the hoopoe foretold of your passage," he declares in a voice that cannot help but sing and chant even as he speaks. He does not search for his words, but he does have an accent.

"Our people are undergoing a period of great poverty. Our hospitality will be modest, but we all know of your love of knowledge. The knowledge of Qoum is very ancient, and we would like to share certain aspects of it with you. Our country begins just within the dunes, not far beyond the pass. Would you accept our invitation to visit tomorrow morning, without ceremony? Your presence and that of your lady-in-waiting will suffice to honor us."

"It is with great joy that I will discover the desert and the encampment where your people live," replies the queen.

With pride the old man corrects her. "It is more than an encampment! For centuries our people have built and maintained actual cities according to principles founded in ancient wisdom. And while we may be in a dormant period at present, our glory shall return!"

"Do not heed that old man's ramblings," says the caravan leader. "The land of Qoum is completely buried in the sand, there is nothing worthy of interest there, even less so of your visit."

"Allow me to be the judge of my interest," replies the queen. "Continue, therefore, to leave to the women the task of replying to this respectable man! Tomorrow morning, you will undertake the preparation of the embassy we are expecting. You will alone and uninterrupted. You need no longer concern yourself with our repose or desires, nor should you feel guilty, as in this very instant, for forgetting to bring us something to drink, and to our guest as well!"

Caught in a flagrant breach of the laws of hospitality, the caravan leader sends a murderous gaze in the young woman's direction, chewing the edge of his short dry mustache with such rage that he bites his lip.

"Queen Bilqis," says the old man, "do not, for a glass of water, compromise all that your patience has constructed throughout these weeks. I am refreshed by the very concern you show for my thirst. It is almost night; I shall spend it by the fire with the guides and the camel drivers. We will leave tomorrow before sunrise."

"That is out of the question!" exclaims the caravan leader. "Everything here is under my authority and I will not allow it! The queen cannot take the risk of venturing into the desert with an old man as her sole escort. How do I know this is not a trap, that you will not hand her over to tribes that wish to abduct her to obtain a fabulous ransom?"

"Who says it is not a trap? I do," replies the old man, pulling himself almost straight to confront the caravan leader. "How dare you doubt my honor and scorn the hospitality of my people! You are so accustomed to scheming and calculating that the simplest and purest intentions, which your queen recognizes naturally, immediately seem suspicious to you. My poor child."

"I am not your child!" shouts the leader.

"But others are," replies the old man, looking around him with a circular gaze.

The discussion has attracted all the other men, causing them to stop what they are doing. The men of the desert stand to the fore: some of them reply proudly, "Yes, he is our uncle." They recognize him as a kinsman, someone who cannot be mocked without the one scorning him risking a bloody vengeance. The caravan leader is now confronted with an unexpected turn of events. He does not know how to deal with it, nor is he quite sure what the rules are. He only knows that he cannot oppose all these men at once.

"Share then your children's meal and their hearth this night," he says disdainfully. "And take the queen with you tomorrow, since that is what she wants. But be back here before the sun has reached the middle of the sky! You will have to make the return journey in the heat of the day, but no one, I believe, would like to endanger our embassy to Bakhit."

"We shall return by then."

The old man gives his word with due solemnity before withdrawing to a corner of the camp, surrounded by the men who have come forward as his companions.

The queen is satisfied by the outcome of the discussion, even if the aggravating discord with the caravan leader is a source of concern. The night is falling quickly. She lets herself be guided to the place set aside for her; she passes through the bundles scattered here and there, among the shelters being erected, and the men rushing to and fro.

"Nour, the old man says he was warned of our arrival by the hoopoe? Which hoopoe is that?" she asks, following a servant who frays a passage through the commotion and the crowd.

"The bird that chose to live for some time in your little courtyard, Bilqis The hoopoe is Solomon's envoy. She must have stopped off here as we have, on her way to Jerusalem."

The queen accepts Nour's words without betraying her astonishment. She does not wish to disturb this world so close to the gods, with whom Nour seems able to communicate so naturally.

The journey to the land of Qoum is a peaceful one, full of new sensations for the queen: the slow rocking on the camel's back where she is safely attached to the saddle, balancing precariously, the heady feeling of dominating an immense landscape without ever losing sight of the fragility of her own situation, at the mercy of any sudden and unpredictable movement on the part of the camel. The queen has already ridden a camel, just outside her palace, but not while venturing into unknown territory. She is now moving off into a seemingly unending landscape, and it is impossible for her to measure their progress. Only the old man knows; he walks on ahead, leading the queen's camel, followed by Nour, who is also on camelback and surrounded by the three guards the caravan leader insisted on sending with them. The little company enters the dunes. They lose their bearings deep within the desert sands. Through this golden dust, which gives out far greater wealth than any that can be accumulated in the coffers of the kingdom, the queen journeys toward new conquests, the only ones her master taught her to view as indispensable. She draws near the place where she anticipates enigmas are transformed, perhaps even solved.

Through the fine veil protecting her she can make out the first signs of an ancient human presence: in this landscape entirely of curves, there are now straight lines, walls of baked earth rising from the sand of a warmer, redder color. The old man stops. He has no more strength and is losing his balance. Somehow he manages to make the queen's camel bend down on its knees; he jiggles the bridle with which he has been leading the beast and coaxes the animal with his voice. He uses strong words and has no need to shout.

They have arrived at the entrance to the city. Nothing is moving, no one has come to meet them. With their feet sinking deep into the sand, they walk the few feet that separates them from the top of the dune. From that point they can make out a hollow that is wider than the others, as if the hand of a god had flattened one or two dunes to carve out an almost plane surface amid the sandy hills. From there they can see the entire city as a tracing, as if it were a diagram drawn on the ground. Several groups of buildings take up the space and are interconnected by low walls with small openings. These are not mere enclosures but actual houses, long rectangles joined together in a grid of "house-streets," where two circular groups hold the dominant position on either side of the wide ravine. More majestic edifices shelter there, protected by a succession of concentric walls. Rising above them all is a dome with an oval orifice at its center, from which vertical poles—the extremities of two ladders—emerge to rise toward the sky: these are the only entrance to the dome, which has no other opening towards the outside.

The moment they reach the top of the dune, a gentle sound calls them, steady even in its own quiet insistence, a generous litany inviting contemplation, an attentive listening to a world uninterrupted by constant action. At first the queen tries to ignore the monotonous chant emanating from the dome, to banish it as if it were some misplaced transposition of her family misfortune in the heart of the desert. For her, this voice is her mother's before it became strange, before it rose into a shrill shriek to be lost in a register of boundless pain. Here the woman's voice is well-tempered, and it holds the regular rhythm of the melody through a steady scansion of the words, words that also sound familiar to the queen, although their meaning escapes her.

"Boetslala ah ah tsala tsala boitsala..."

She is filled with fear, the same fear she felt as a little girl the first time she heard her mother sing like this, standing by the small altar with its fire lit to the unknown god, a fire that had also frightened her since Ishta had first threatened her with its burning embers.

"Life is an eternal beginning, a perpetual reconstruction over the ruins of a never-ending time," says the old man. "That is the meaning of the chant that rises above our town: It never stops from sunrise to sunset. It upholds the principle of our existence, that time is continuity, it extends beyond the beginning and the end of the day, beyond birth and death. The past is a passage preserved in memory to enable each of us to accomplish, in the present, the task that falls to us."

"I recognize that voice," murmurs the queen. She is suddenly overwhelmed by the heat and the crushing weight of the sun's rays, from which nothing protects them in this place perched high above the town.

"We all recognize it. Qoum is the point of departure for all life, the place where all people are born. In the center of the town, the walls meet and form a square that surrounds a sacred pool. For the time being it is hidden by drought under a thick cracking crust, but in the early days the waters regularly filled it. One day the first man rose out of the silt at the center of the pool. Woman appeared with the next rainstorm. They built the town and populated it, and their descendants moved on to other regions to give birth to other nations, never to look back. Today the town sleeps, but it keeps watch over the pool, the place of an anticipated rebirth, and over these ruined walls that shall be rebuilt when the cycle of time passes this way once again."

"I recognize that voice, but it is not my own, it is that of Ishta, the woman who gave birth to me although she did not want to, a woman who refuses to call herself a mother, who imprisons me in her misery…"

"Leave the past behind! Destroy what it has left and use the material it has left you to build your own house! Look at these concentric buildings set around the central dome, three rings each consisting of several homes. They have been built from the outside toward the inside, according to the succession of time: when the central ring is full, the new city-dwellers move on to the outermost circle, choosing an abandoned dwelling. Then they build their own houses on top of those ruins whose history they preserve and protect. And the house-streets obey the same principle: to keep moving forward, to find their place in walls which others who have moved elsewhere have abandoned. When they reach the outermost point, they turn back as if they were making a new departure, a clear and direct return to the source, not a painful passage back through each stage of the past. The chant helps us with this: a melody cannot be sung from back to front. Sing and you will see, everything will become simple. Sing! Find your voice!"

Without further explanation, the old man heads slowly down to the first circle of houses at a rather hesitant pace: He begins with his stick, then his left foot, and immediately afterward, his right foot. As he turns his steps toward the source of the music, his deep voice picks up the melody. He hesitates for a moment before finding the right note, then he holds it. His breath is astonishingly full and continuous, before quietly joining in with the female voice as it guides him further up the scale. Leaning on his stick, he pauses for a moment, then stands up straight and turns to look at the queen. He makes no gesture, but his gaze is full of an imperious will and scorn for anyone who might refuse his invitation. He continues to hold long notes at the limit of his breath, forcing his voice in order to incite the queen to join him. She accepts, heading after him slowly down the steep slope of the dune, along the merest suggestion of a path. After further hesitation and another mute urging from the old man, she tries to find the note. With her mouth closed, she tries to follow the litany. Until this moment, she has only joined in the lighthearted melodies that are sung by women among themselves or at weddings; never has a female voice accompanied the sacred invocations in the temples. Finally, she opens her mouth and allows the sound to escape: what comes out seems so far from the chant of the model! They have reached the middle of the slope, where the sand has formed a sort of ledge, and the old man comes back a few steps to stand next to her: "Try to sing. Try again! Don't imitate; try to find the voice inside of yourself. Go back to your own source."

The light suddenly becomes blinding. The landscape vanishes behind the heat-shimmer of a thick desert mist, and they encounter a thick cloud of whiteness. Even the music seems less clear, it sounds confused and transformed. The queen can hear footsteps, crunching, the first the heavy steps of armed warriors moving across the sand, then the lighter, almost skipping steps of a woman who appears before them dressed in a long white gown with gilded tassels, her head crowned by a metal diadem embedded with fine, multicolored jewels. The tip of each of the three points rising from the crown is set with black stones. The woman glides hurriedly along the path, followed by the warriors. With no further thought for the old man or Nour, Bilqis steps behind her quickly, so as not to lose her in the thick fog. At the bottom of the dune, a tall boulder blocks the path. An awning has been carved into it, beneath which is a wooden door. The woman with the diadem takes a key from her belt, opens the door, and turns to the warrior standing nearest her. Bilqis recognizes her father, and then the diadem: she has seen the crown only once, in a carved wooden box that Ishta had opened one day when she was calm and had evaded the evil spirits. She showed her daughter the diadem that her mother had worn, like her mother's mother before her, according to the customs of the land where she was from.

Ishta appears on the threshold of the door carved into the stone: her long face has no wrinkles, and her thick curls, not yet gone gray with suffering, fall to her shoulders in a riot of disheveled agitation; her enormous eyes are open wide, pleading, and traces of tears still mark her cheeks beneath her prominent cheekbones. On seeing Ishta, the woman with the diadem vanishes into the mist, leaving the jewels, the sign of her royalty, on the threshold. Bilqis' father, the king who has come from Sheba to the edge of the world in order to reopen the caravan route, bends over to pick up the diadem. He reaches out to Ishta, motions as if to place it on her head. Ishta trembles and cries out, then returns abruptly to the depths of the cave. Bilqis steps forward and stands before her father at the cave's entrance: her hair is tightly gathered beneath her veil into a wide round chignon on the top of her head, as if it had been thus planned deliberately for their meeting. The hoopoe emerges from the fog, from the direction where the woman disappeared. On its head is the same feathered ornament with three points set with black at the tip. *Ooop, oop, oop.* The bird flies over the king and his daughter to the entrance of the cave, decides not to enter, then flies off again. Bilqis follows his colorful flight with her gaze.

As the bird passes, the white fog breaks open and dissolves, revealing what it had kept hidden. The hoopoe flies above the old man, his guards, and the woman with the diadem, who is now covered with a dark blue veil through which only the center of her face is visible:

Nour was wearing just such a veil this morning! But it can't be, she cannot be the woman with the diadem.

Yet it is Nour! Visions and reality grow confused, they become impossible to distinguish. Bilqis searches for her father and the men who were with him: everything has vanished. She can feel the weight of the diadem on her head, but when she reaches for it with her hand, there is nothing there but the cloth covering her and, lodged in her hair, a colored, black-tipped feather. The opening she stands before does not lead into a rock, but into the wall of the first concentric circle.

The chanting chimes out again. The column consisting of the old man, Nour, and their escorts has reached the bottom of the hill and continues implacably on its way. As she follows them through the first wall, Bilqis easily picks up the hymn; the words form in her mouth even though she does not understand them. The sound rises, resonating loud and strong within her. It emerges to form part of the melody directed toward an unknown destination.

What gods are venerated in this country?

Her whole body is possessed by this chant without a beginning or end; it fills her with energy, roots her to the earth, where she steps lightly, her body floating outside of ordinary sensations. The heat has grown stronger and stronger as the sun rises to its zenith, but it no longer overwhelms her. Sweat trickles along her temples, but she no longer feels thirsty. Grains of sand are lodged between her foot and the straps of her sandal, and while they irritate her heel and the sole of her foot, this no longer hinders her step.

They are moving toward the source of the melody, toward the heart of the circles. They walk along an alleyway between two houses, then emerge again under the open sky, into the space separating the first two rings: there is earth here, and a palm tree watches over the memory of a time when water flowed toward the little rivulets dug between two squares of earth. But now everything has become desolate from drought, it is all cracked and compressed. And yet there is still life, as is confirmed by the sound of the voice that is coming closer and the odor of incense wafting toward them. They stand opposite the dome with its whitewashed walls, completely smooth and without openings; a frieze runs shoulder-high around the walls, and a thousand sculpted eyes look at them, scrutinizing and weighing. The old man has stopped singing.

"We will go no farther," he declares. "Only those who will devote themselves, from this moment on, to the rebirth of man are allowed to enter. It is elsewhere that you shall follow your path toward truth. Look straight ahead, with your eyes open. But beware! Not everyone is capable of seeing the truth, of confronting it. To accept the truth is also to carry it without seeking to rid oneself of it or to fling it back at others not capable of hearing it. Truth is like your voice, it is within that you will find it; others can only bring you elements of your quest. Truth is a treasure, but it cannot be handed out freely any more than the song of Qoum can be heard in any circumstances. He who forgets this rule stands apart, loses his ability to adjust, and will sink into madness. Keep watch over yourself, and a divine blessing will cover you with its shadow, it will protect you from the excesses of the sun, who is but a magnanimous god. You can see the effects here!"

"But who is this god? Whom do you honor in this place?"

"Find the answer that suits you and that suits your people. And remember this place and its song. When your consciousness grows dim and you are overwhelmed by parasitical thoughts, retire to your chambers and let yourself be carried by the time without end to where the song leads you. Search for the right note, and you will find your voice."

Bilqis is striding forward with her head held high along the path from the town. First she walks into the sands, without sinking in too deeply, then with the help of the guides, she climbs onto her camel. Her body effortlessly follows the rhythm of the long, regular steps. She is no longer tossed and shaken as she was on the way here. Her body no longer has the consistency of a soft sack without structure and is not subjected now to the caprices of the terrain and the animals' movements. Her head no longer wobbles in every direction. She follows the cadence with dignity, sitting high and straight. The animal has become an extension of herself, enabling her to move forward without having to think about it. Nothing weighs down her spirit; she is free of obsessions and devotes herself to the sensation of the moment. She belongs to the dunes where she directs her gaze, surrendering to the gust of the warm wind as it presses her clothes against her skin and makes her feel as if she were cutting through a block of pure heat.

The sun reaches its zenith when they are in sight of their camp. Bakhit is already there, sitting outside the royal tent. The two flaps of the tent's embroidered canopy are open wide: The queen should have been seated between their symmetrical curves to receive Bahkit, and yet it was the lord of the desert who watched over the tent and who rose to greet the new arrivals. The caravan leader stands next to him, his spear in hand, as if waiting to stab the old man the moment they arrive. Bakhit goes over to the old man, who is walking next to the queen's camel. He leads him to the seat on his left, and when he passes in front of the caravan leader, he lifts the threatening weapon to a vertical position with a slight, but firm, gesture. He then bows deeply to the queen, and the moment she dismounts, she returns the greeting. She nods and accepts the support of his hand to walk up the slight platform where their chairs have been arranged. The servants bring each of them a pitcher containing water freshly drawn from the well.

After a brief conversation with the old man in an unknown tongue, Bakhit turns directly to the queen: "I have sent to you the lord and guardian of Qoum, the land of my ancestors. He has conveyed to me the purity of your intentions and the proof of the justice of your mission. On arriving here I was greeted by another sign: this tent, closed by a purple and crimson brocade curtain. It already appeared in the Book, the one Solomon's people hand down from generation to generation; it has sheltered the tablets of law set down by his god, the sign of their covenant. Make haste therefore to the place you must go. My personal guard will accompany your caravan to ease your passage through the world of sands."

Then, turning to the caravan leader, who stands stiffly at their side with a haughty, rigid attitude, Bakhit adds, "Continue your duty at the queen's side by seeking advice from those I place at your side. But refrain henceforth from misjudging for the sake of appearances!"

Chapter eight

P iero sees Bakhit, and in his mind he is already painting him. The man of the desert is wearing a long, floating robe,
cinched at the waist with a belt, and his head is covered with a
turban. His clothing is the same as that of the old lord of
Qoum, Bilqis' guide to the buried city, but while the old man's
clothes are threadbare, wrinkled and torn.Bakhit's are new, cut
from the finest pieces of cloth, those that Benedetto della Fran-
cesca selected from among the Florentine woolens—fabrics im-
ported from France, cottons and silks from the East. Piero loves
the feel of fine fabric, the way it falls as well as its sharp, slightly
acrid scent that fills the back rooms of his father's shop. He
walks among the shelves, his hand reaching out to feel the edge
of each bolt of cloth; he rolls it between his thumb and his other
fingers to evaluate the quality and the texture; he caresses the
top of the bolt with his palm and, from time to time, pulls a
sample into the light to gauge the depth of blue, the softness of
ivory, or the rich brilliance of pink.

For Bakhit he selects a heavy, sand-colored cotton, which
is thick and tightly woven to wrap the figurine he uses as a
model. He will work on the flowing movement of the thick fabric draped around the hips, the play of light and shadow in each
fold, the man's stature, proud and firm, enhanced by the flowing garment. Bakhit stands before Piero, and the artist can see
him, but he cannot visualize the background against which Sil-

via's story has set him. To Piero, a world without water or trees can have no true existence; he cannot resign himself to limiting the background of a painting to horizons as bleak as those Silvia has described. And yet he has read descriptions of such places in books: when he began work on the portrait of Saint Jerome, his friend Giovanni Bacci found him a copy of an ancient chronicle of a journey through the East. Using this description, Piero began by reducing the saint's surroundings to a few rocky walls of a pinkish ocher beneath a uniformly blue sky. The composition seemed frightenly bland: what man on earth could feel moved in a spiritual way in such a uniformly desolate place? To raise one's eyes to the sky and study it with the intensity of a Saint Jerome --- the earth must inspire a dialogue with everything that extends beyond it; nature must rejoice, trees must bloom abundantly for man to feel the desire to enrich his inner world and turn toward the heavens. That is the beauty Piero has sought to recreate in churches in the hope that it will inspire the faithful—rich and poor alike, humble or powerfulto surpass themselves as do the saints

Gradually, he added a touch of green to the background of the painting, then a building of pinkish roughcast to establish a connection between the grass and the rocks, the gray tinted with orange. Then, at the center of the image, he dug deep into the ground, creating a shape filled with water, and he was unable to resist the pleasure of accentuating the depth with a shimmer of reflections. Whenever Piero finds himself at the edge of a lake or a pond, another vision of nature appears in the water's reflection: The colors become denser, the darkness of the lake's depths makes the surroundings more intense, the reflection of the sun's rays creates brilliant effects on the water, sparkling with precious gold. The treetops plunge from the sky to the water, and their branches form a carpet of delicately woven leaves that ripple gently with the wind as much as with the currents that ruffle the surface of the water. Piero leans forward; he feels drawn, as if he is about to be pulled into the water. He would like to dive in and swim across this moving surface, to penetrate the interior of this aquatic world and become part of its mirrored painting. He has discovered a similar passion among the Flemish artists, whose paintings go for a great price among the princes of the north of Italy. It is not that he is envious, but eager to observe and know more. He has spent hours gazing at the paintings of Van der Weyden that Leonello d'Este, the Marquis of Ferrara, acquired, and Piero has gradually adopted the techniques that the painter from Tournai to transfer the mirror image onto a flat surface, softening the natural elements overlooking and surrounding the body of water. Inside the chestnut grove where he has set his Saint Jerome, he has depicted, on either side of the natural pond, a meandering river, which enlivens the left-hand side of the picture, while allowing a smooth transition from the foreground to the background. To do his penance, Jerome has turned his back on the beauties of the natural world that nurture and support him. He has followed the movement of the tree and created a new link between earth and sky. The magnificence of the setting lends a new significance to the saint's asceticism: it is as if Jerome were submitting with pleasure and delight to the world described by the painter, all the better thereafter to find the strength and desire to renounce it. Piero is fond of the color red, hence his decision to set on the ground, in front of Jerome, who is absorbed in silent contemplation, the cardinal's hat which the pope had given him. The saint was able to refuse material goods and honors because he already possessed them.

Piero has no desire to paint men in rags in a world in ruins. He takes his models from antiquity, where there are sound examples of ideally proportioned architecture, with carefully sculpted columns and capitals, balanced peristyles and tympanums, rectangular temples and statues celebrating the beauty of the human body. How can man subsist in an environment where the sand covers everything, where the domes that serve as monuments are sinking into the ground? How can one be content to meditate in the midst of a uniform, monotonous succession of sand dunes, of desert hills that may appear graceful in their undulations, but are crushed beneath a harsh light without nuances, and in a place where the contrast between the folds deep in shadow and the sun-drenched slopes is so brutal? The mathematical rigor of Piero's mind rebels against a world where space revolves on itself beneath a domed vault and in an endless spiraling of concentric rings, where time is distended to the infinity of a linear chant devoid of rhythm. Such a world eludes the convergent and divergent lines Piero draws so patiently to determine the vanishing point and the equilibrium. It resists any calculation of angles or rational determination of proportion. The void, the space one must leave around each figure to allow it to move and assert its existence, must be filled with a true presence, an inner order conquering the profusion of the world. Were a man to let go, he could lose his integrity and his identity, the dignity which God has given to all those who believe.

What Piero remembers best of the story Silvia just told him is the final image: Bakhit seated on a majestic throne. Piero will cover the sides and the seat with a blue fabric, accentuating the folds of Bakhit's sand-colored robe. The old man is now holding a gold-tipped cane, a mark of his power. He turns to the queen, who is standing before him; his face softened and ennobled by his two-pointed gray beard. He looks at her with a kind and gentle, but distant, expression: is he really concentrating his attention on her, or is he deeply immersed in the silence of his inner world?

"I'm cold," Silvia murmurs. The canvases stretched along the sides of the carriage, a precarious cabin, echo the sound, and her muffled complaint resonates like a cry in the dense silence: only a few seconds ago her voice rang out abruptly, following upon the rumbling of the wheels, the metallic clanking of the axle, and the constant grinding of the wooden wheels against the bumpy road. From the moment they left Borgo, Silvia's story has been frequently interrupted by the squeaking of the carriage and the vibration of her own voice with each lurch of the carriage: the road to Monterchi is far from smooth. Some of her words have been swallowed, fragments of sentences remained unfinished, but Piero has not asked her to repeat herself: he is no longer within their present flight, but at the very heart of the story—with the queen, in the palanquin tossed this way and that by the mules. He does not regret that he chose to go with Silvia in this uncomfortable, almost ridiculous cariole—a luxurious and incongruous gift from the prince of Urbino— instead of riding on his own, as he usually does. Piero is squeezed next to Silvia on the carriage's single seat, their cushions placed side by side to share the journey of the desert queen. Images and sensations have filled the gaps between the words, going beyond meaning.

The story becomes a brutal reality when the cariole suddenly lurches to one side, then shakes in every direction, swinging from left to right in a movement that throws the occupants together. Then the iron cabin is propelled forward. They are almost thrown out onto the team of horses, while the coachman, shouting loudly, tries to restrain the beasts and bring them to a halt. The horses are slipping toward the edge of the slope, in danger of losing their footing entirely at any moment and sliding off the path. The noise, tumult, screams, creaking, rumbling, and dull thudding of wood and metal grow ever louder until, in the moment that follows, there is a more violent shaking than all the others, and all movement suddenly ceases; a crushing silence falls over them.

It is amidst this silence that Silvia's voice rings out, "I'm cold!" Piero, by her side, hears her complaint. It seems so strange following the peril they have just experienced. His reaction is even more unexpected.

"How can you be cold in the midst of so much heat!"

He is still immersed in the heat of the desert. It takes him a moment to feel the weight of the two cloaks laid over his shoulders and of the blanket across his knees. Men's voices are again calling out around the horses. Piero sits up, turns, and unfastens the pieces of cloth protecting the side of the carriage. Through the frame thus created—an acute angle and two symmetrical half-circles—a line of dense black trees appears, scarcely separated from the road by a verge covered in snow. This natural barrier fills all the space so that he cannot imagine anything beyond it except another row of trees, then another, and another after that, like the sand dunes in the infinite space of the desert. But is this not an illusion created by the limited field of vision between the two pieces of cloth? *Is it the frame that determines what the eye sees, or is it the eye of the painter that predetermines the frame and sets off the space to be filled by the painting?*

Piero steps out of the carriage like a robot. He pushes aside the servants who run up to tell him the cause of the incident and turn it into a drama: A tree trunk was blocking the road. If the fog had not lifted…if the road had not been straight…if the coachman's attention had not been drawn to the road by a family of rodents crossing ahead of them…if his shout had not sounded the alarm to a rider who was more alert than the others and who immediately conveyed the message behind him…the carriage would have hurtled into the obstacle, the carts carrying the other servants, their luggage, and their supplies, would have crashed into each other, and all the horses accompanying this ill-assorted procession would have panicked. God alone knows in what state the travelers might now have been!

"Praise be to Saint Francis our protector!" murmur the most devout among them—or those who wish appear devout—as they cross themselves. "Good health to those damned rats, which crossed the road at the right time!" exclaim others laughing noisily as a bottle they had spirited away from one of the crates is passed around as if it were a trophy.

Piero pays no attention at all to the fallen tree. He does not feel the biting cold and remains insensitive to the servants' agitation as they hurry to chop up the trunk blocking their way.

He does not even think of adding his great strength to theirs. He has never been concerned by material problems: If Silvia were to ask, or Mario were to suggest that he help, then he would have gone without hesitation; he would have found the most ingenious method to pull the massive piece of wood out of the way without too great an effort in the same manner that he solves the complex problem of setting up the scaffolding inside a church. But if no one claims his attention, he does not see, he does not hear, and he leaves the work to those who can, quite efficiently, do it in his place.

He walks up and down the path looking for the angle from which his gaze will once again capture the forest in all its depth and from where he will be able to observe the shifting line of the treetops as the distance separating him from his goal increases: Is it not the painter's eye which defines the term, the limit of the field, the point of departure for the vanishing lines? Should he not go even farther than Alberti, go beyond his definition of the frame and remove the viewpoint from the window in which Alberti has enclosed it, in order to trace the lines on which the painting's measurements are based using mathematical models and figures? Piero does not quite yet know what he is trying to accomplish, what it is he is feeling, or what is troubling him.

"Maestro, Maestro, don't wander too far off! There are brigands in the region!"

"And we don't have Bakhit's men to protect us," Piero thinks, still absorbed by the story that belongs as much to him now as it does to Silvia. He walks up to the highest point, to the place where the road begins to drop down again. Perched high on one of the numerous hills surrounding them, the village of Monterchi can be seen in the distance. A patch of blue in the dreary sky directs a ray of light upon the roofs of the houses, spilling down the hillsides to the white stone wall. Brick red, soft ocher, bluish-gray, light brown; square towers, slanted roofs, openings shaped like the crenellations of the fortifications:

what a relief it is to see the colors and the juxtaposition of familiar shapes once again—a space not enclosed, but limited, which changes with the rhythm of his steps and his gaze.

The chiming of the church bells is carried on the wind, over the forest, to where Piero is walking. It scans the hours, giving a clear rhythm to the passing time. But it does not stretch time into infinity, and this fills Piero with fear: *What is man's place in a time that has neither beginning nor end?* Piero is not tormented by the question of salvation. He is not frightened by what lurks beyond this life in which he feels profoundly rooted. He places his trust in God, that He will not ask more of him than he can endure. It is not what he might find in the afterlife that fills him with dread, but what he might *not* find. He finds it unbearable that the world after death might resemble the ruins and emptiness of the city of Qoum. It is a source of genuine pleasure for him to make skillfully designed interiors, harmoniously balanced arcades and porticos, mathematically accurate perspectives founded on the geometry of sumptuous floorings; to dress men and women in rich and luminously colored cloths that drape perfectly; to make their faces vibrate with restrained, silent emotion. This universe of beauty and harmony is the only vision he might propose of a heavenly Jerusalem, of the palace where God will receive the righteous upon their death.

Crows fly overhead, squawking. The black birds scatter, then they return to perch on the surrounding trees. Their shrill cries seem like an evil omen to Piero: "No one can attain infinity without submitting to the trial of death." The words he heard during a meeting of humanists at the Palazzo Bacci come back to him, wheeling in his mind like the ebony birds in the sky and banishing all other thoughts. He shivers. The village of Monterchi has disappeared into the fog; the landscape is buried in snow, beneath a hovering mist, and now seems dark and ominous as if something were about to emerge from deep within the valleys, from the heart of the gray and brown gloom. The trees seem frozen as if contaminated by some mineral rigidity: as if a mere shift in viewpoint or a change in the light would be enough to suggest the imminent, ineluctable judgment of God.

Two troops of men suddenly emerge at the same moment from either side of Piero's procession—they are armed men. They rush at each other in the heart of the valley: horsemen and foot soldiers, men trapped in heavy armor, soldiers wearing colored doublets and no other protection than the heavy sword and dagger in their hands, heralds carrying banners and blowing trumpets that echo discordantly. Standards with martial emblems of black eagles and vengeful dragons unfurl against the sky. Spears and arrows fly, helmets of every shape and color clash together, intermingling and flashing with the slightest burst of light. Faces remain inscrutable and determined, staring at the death they will bring, but refusing to contemplate their own demise. There are those who see the enemy's blade draw near their bared throat, and they cry out, mouth wide open, in pain and surprised desperation. A white horse appears from the left. The horseman on its back, torso and legs covered in armor, has a face distorted by a grimace that portends no mercy. In his right hand he grips a heavy mace, and with his left hand, he guides his horse. The moment they enter the fray, the horse rears up…

It is always at this same point in his dream that Piero starts and awakes. Normally he sits bold upright on his bed, sweating, his eyes wide with terror. He can feel the shock, the violence of his body being thrown to the ground, and above his head he can see the horse's legs about to crush him. He has frequently had this nightmare of a violent death during a brutal battle. The valley beneath the village of Monterchi has often provided the imaginary setting to his dream.

"The world is closed, our dreams are not": how often has he heard these words in the same calm, poised, self-assured voice in the course of an evening of debate at the Bacci palazzo.

The words are etched upon his memory: they go with him everywhere and have become a part of him just like the images that take shape in his works, emerging from the stories he hears, the people he meets, the emotions that arise from a place, the dreams that pursue him. He concedes that science enables painting to go beyond appearances and attain reality, yet unlike Alberti, he cannot contain everything within the frame of a window or allow what is mathematically accurate to remove that which belongs to the imagination. Perspective is there to give rhythm and proportion to objects within a finite space, so that man can inhabit the place where he belongs and transcend the material nature of things through the power of his mind. The battle has faded away. Smoke rises in the distance from the middle of a field. This brings Piero back to the reality of their journey, to that other form of death—the plague—and to the stakes at the outskirts of the villages they passed through, where the only people to be seen were ghostlike figures flitting quickly from place to place.

He has obeyed Silvia's injunction, abandoning his family home to flee from the hideous mask of death: he dreads this passage through a world of suffering, where all beauty is destroyed in the contortion of mangled bodies.

He lives in fear of everything that is becoming dislocated and destroyed.

"Maestro, Maestro, look!" Piero turns around, following the gestures of the servants who have been running after him. Their hands, still carrying their axes, are pointing to something a hundred yards below them, something lost in a halo of mist that he cannot make out.

"Look, the trunk has been cut up, the passage is free!" He knows that is expected to leave his thoughts behind, to show his interest and congratulate them.

"Let us hurry before the fog obscures everything."

"But master, the fog has lifted, there is no more danger!"

Yet a bank of fog obscures his vision, blocking the carriage from view. He cannot see whether Silvia is still huddled inside or whether she has decided to climb out. Piero walks back to her, and the fear he began to feel on the hilltop gradually loosens its grip. He returns to Silvia as to a spring revealing his reflection, as to something he dares not call "love." Is love not the force that constantly takes him back to her, the feeling that he is where he belongs when he is by her side despite the constant urge to be elsewhere? Is love not the impetus of the desire to break the curse, to see, at last, her hips grow round and her belly ripple with the movement of the tiny unborn life? He returns to Silvia as he returns to the source of the story that has been carrying them from the moment she ventured to tell it to him: the queen of the South has become their companion, and her quest has become his, challenging him to the very depths of his helplessness to accept with serenity the vast, unlimited nature of things.

Where did Silvia come upon the material? Who was her source? She had mentioned a monk who returned from a long stay in the Eastern lands; but how could a Franciscan be interested in the community of Qoum—waiting for man's rebirth at the heart of the desert, honoring no god in particular and respecting the freedom of every nation to choose the god that suits it. Silvia has been Piero's wife for many years now, and yet feels as though he does not really know her any better than on the first day she appeared before him by the fountain, the day she answered his offer of marriage by submitting to the will of God. In many ways she has remained what she was then: a child from nowhere, her essence hidden, the way Nour's mysterious essence is hidden from Bilqis. Piero returns to her side as to a fascinating stranger.

Silvia immediately feels the cold, biting air from outside the moment Piero lifts up the flap to the carriage. His abrupt movement has caught the cloth in the structure and it has not been pulled back down. Shivering, Silvia reaches up for the flap, struggling against the three layers of blankets covering her: the cold assails her, piercing her flesh. Fortunately, Mario runs forward to anticipate her gesture, "Stay inside, *Signora*, it's freezing! Don't worry, it will only take a moment."

She slumps back onto the cushions with a sudden weariness; she has never felt like this before, has always refused to be intimidated by her physical needs, to yield to weakness or to complain, even from the cold. What has come over her? Fatigue submerges her as if she had been walking in the desert for several days. She closes her eyes. A wolf is howling in the distance. A shiver runs through her. Is it fever? Is it fear of the wolf? But how can she be afraid when she is only a few miles from Gubbio, the place where Saint Francis transformed the terrifying animal into our "brother wolf," and praised God for "our sister death"? Silvia slips into a sort of doze where all the images blur together: the wolf is running across the desert and catches up with Bilqis at the top of the dune, when she discovers the city of Qoum, and the hoopoe flies above the city, dazzling...

Piero climbs into the carriage. It is difficult for him to fit his long limbs into the tight cabin. He takes up nearly all the room, angling his feet between the cushions and the edge of the wooden shell. He is squeezed tightly against Silvia and tries to find the position they had adopted earlier during the journey, with her head in the hollow of his shoulder, their ribs aligned, and his hip curved into the hollow of her waist. Sitting so closely together reinforces the intimacy of their reading, the impression that the world she draws them into actually belongs to them, and to them alone.

As he climbs back into the carriage, Piero is surprised that Silvia shows no physical reaction: she has always been so careful to remain mistress of herself and her surroundings. He takes hold of her hand under the blanket. It is hot, almost burning. He squeezes it tightly, tenderly. "Don't be afraid, I'm here," he murmurs.

No, truthfully, she is not afraid—of wolves or of death. She is simply very tired; she places her head against Piero's shoulder to still the sound of dull thudding and the throbbing pain. She surrenders in a way she has never been able to before and falls into a deep sleep.

An atmosphere of peace enfolds them as they make their way toward the plain: even the metallic rattle and creaking wood of the carriage, which was not meant for long journeys, become less strident, and the cold loosens its grip for a time. Now that the earlier fright has passed, the danger they escaped has tempered the ardor of the driver and the escort. From the moment they left Borgo San Sepolcro they hardly refrained from shoving and singing, joking and making a show of their deliverance: they were escaping from the epidemic, turning their back on death. Now with the accident, they were reminded that death can always take another guise; reminded that the plague, and being trapped in the city, are not the only dangers to human life. Preoccupied and vigilant, they have grown silent again, and when they reach the ford, they remain very calm as they evaluate on the situation, weighing the best means of negotiating their passage.

Recent floods have destroyed the bridge. At the edge of the river, shallow once again, two wooden square blocks remain, the last remnants of the fragile structure. Piero and Silvia climb out of the carriage. They will be the last to cross, once the cariole has been taken to the far side and the horses are harnessed and waiting. Silvia is unsteady on Piero's arm. "It's nothing, just a little malaise, don't worry," she says with effort. And what if the miracle had finally arrived—what if the longed-for child were at last a reality? But the gray shadow veiling Silvia's face belies this happy thought, and another worry takes its place: what if they have brought the plague with them? Above all, they must let nothing show before they have settled in Monterchi. The villagers who have come to help them cross the ford might become alarmed and deny them their refuge at the last moment.

The seat covered with cushions that they used in the cariole has been set up by the remains of the bridge. Silvia slumps wearily onto the narrow bench, collapses, leans towards the wooden pieces as if she wants to touch them. Her hair has been pulled tight on the back of her head with a white cotton Arezzo bonnet, which the Bacci family offered her not long before. This accentuates the hollows in her face, flattening her round cheeks and making her face seem longer than usual. Around them there are no particular signs of anxiety: the hills surround the plain with gentle curves; the village of Monterchi rises just beyond the river, and the joyful cries of children emerge from the houses above. There is life, so near, full of sound after the oppressive silence of the forest. The gray mass of sky has parted in its center and allows a pale lime light to filter through. The tops of two nearby trees seem to be drawn toward this light as their leaves glisten in the brilliance of a few sunbeams.

How tall should I make these trees in comparison to the hills that close off the space? Piero wonders. He begins to make a mental drawing of lines and angles and prepares to reach into his pocket for his notebook, and the charcoal that is constantly escaping the folds of the paper where he places it and leaving a black powder in the pleats of his clothing and on his already smudged fingers. *No,* he thinks to himself, *not now!*

He looks again at Silvia, collapsed on the seat. For once it is urgency that beckons him to the side of life, and not his painting; which can wait.

Silvia says nothing, her eyes stare at the wood but seem to see much farther, into another future, or into another world. Sitting on the riverbank, she takesS a moment for quiet reflection before passing over to the other shore. She can see what is waiting for her. She accepts the vision with calm, whereas Piero, in the face of her serenity, feels a stab of anxiety in his belly. He must break the hold of this mortal dream, bring Silvia back to him, to all that they share, to the journey of the Queen of Sheba whose story she has been telling day after day. He knows one episode of the story, the one told in the *Golden Legend* that inspired the Franciscans for the frescoes of their church in Arezzo. Voragine's text evokes another bridge, another passage across the water, another vision. Piero sits down next to Silvia. She does not seem to notice; she is frozen, leaning towards the earth, in an attitude of consent as much as humility. As if her body were doubly withdrawn—on the riverbank and folded over on itself—and were taking up an unusual amount of room. Ordinarily, the imposing mass of Piero's body would fill the space without his even being aware of it. This time, he must make do with the edge of the seat, moving from the foreground to the background.

"The Queen of Sheba arrives at Solomon's palace," he begins, driven by the urgency to tell the story—the flow must be maintained, whatever the cost, to prevent the danger of Silvia from falling asleep in front of everyone and arousing suspicion that she might be unwell.

"Solomon took thirteen years to build this magnificent palace. The architect used a great quantity of cedar superior to anything the desert queen could possibly imagine. Through the gates of the palace, open wide to greet her, she can see a series of sumptuous halls, their walls paneled with priceless wood and framed with molding encrusted with white or black marble, with ceilings covered with porphyry and serpentine tiles, supported by thick carved and decorated beams, and resting on fluted stone columns with richly sculpted capitals. Wide, high-backed ivory seats wait to offer rest to the visitor. The seats are decorated with sculptures whose shapes are so precise that even from a distance you can see the abundance of animal life portrayed there, with monkeys and peacocks. But to get there you have to overcome a last obstacle: A wooden bridge crosses the moat surrounding the palace. There is something quite special about the bridge. It is made all of a piece, from the trunk of a tree which, it is said, grew out of the seed placed in Adam's mouth just after his death."

Silvia's voice can suddenly be heard, as if it were coming from somewhere other than her sleepy face. With unusual vigor she asserts, "No, the bridge was not at the entrance to the palace! It was not outside the walls, where everyone could see it and walk on it. Solomon was too wise to use the tree in that way, a tree that had resisted every attempt by the master carpenters to reduce it to the state of a simple beam holding up a palace wall. He decided that it would be fitting to preserve it in circumstances as unusual as the rumors which circulated about its origins."

Silvia has recovered some energy; the desire for her version of the story to prevail has overcome her weakness. The maids have covered her with a pile of blankets; she is no longer as cold. She takes over the role of storyteller from Piero, a role she is not ready to relinquish to anyone.

"Bilqis enters the palace with her suite. Servantslead the caravan directly to the outbuildings, along the outside walls. The queen is impressed by the order that reigns in the rooms they pass through: there are no clusters of courtiers standing around at a loss about what to do, no whirlwinds of servants pretending to be busy, no guards slumped at the foot of the doors. They go past a number of men and women whose carefully assigned outfits indicate their rank and position. Everyone seems to have a purpose, a precise task to perform, and no one gives them more than a glance—out of curiosity to be sure, but nothing like the insistent stare which, in Sheba, makes Bilqis feel so ill at ease when she walks along the corridors of her own palace.

"The queen has now arrived at the heart of the labyrinth, the center of the palace. At the entrance she was greeted by a chamberlain in full regalia. Now she is met by a very young maidservant dressed in a long robe that is not draped, but sewn and girdled, and covered with a bolero whose epaulets lift like the feathers on a bird. She leads the queen with her ladies-in-waiting to the women's quarters, where she must change before

the official ceremony. An inner courtyard acts as a border between the official rooms and the more private part of the palace.
A basin occupies the entire central part of the hall, surrounded
by terraced steps covered with a lush abundance of colorful
plants and bushes that obstruct easy passage. A hollowed-out
tree trunk has been placed across the center of the basin to form
a bridge; the tree has not been completely trimmed, and it lies
whole across the surface of the water. The trunk was sawn down
its entire length and has been scooped out like a boat; short
planks of wood placed along the bottom provide a flat walkway
and make it possible to cross without getting one's feet wet. At
the entrance where the queen is standing, two square piles ensure the bridge is firmly moored. On the other side, the moor-
ing is unique: the end of the trunk, which was once raised towards the sky, is now embedded in the base of a white marble
fountain. At the point where the trunk becomes too narrow to
serve as a bridge, a semi-circular footbridge has been added.
One can reach the other shore by going around the fountain to
the left or to the right.

"The queen pauses to observe the unusual sight—this
fallen tree floating on a transparent substance where visitors can
see their faces and forms reflected. She sees herself in this mirror, as do the servants standing in a group behind her, murmuring and chattering. It is all so new and unexpected! Nour stands
back and looks behind, toward the room they have just left—
ever the watchman, ever mindful of what might come from an
unexpected direction and represent a possible threat. Suddenly,
over the translucent surface of the basin, the majestic tree stands
upright. It grows rigid, and throws off the branches that had
formed its crown. On either side of the trunk, a third of the way
from the top, planks of another wood transform it into a cross.
A man is hanging there by his hands and feet; his body is blood-
ied and tortured, and the queen sees this with fright and pity.
Above his head, which is crowned with thorns, a small tablet has
been nailed; it bears an inscription in an unknown alphabet and

language. The queen cannot make out one single letter, and yet the meaning is embedded within her: "Jesus, King of the Jews." A fire breaks out behind the cross, and through the flames the Temple appears, the masterpiece built by Solomon that she saw on her way to the palace. The Temple is burning, the rows of porticos come crashing down one by one; cries of terror can sometimes be heard above the roar and crackling of the flames; the bursting of wood, the rending asunder of stones ...

"Suddenly it is calm again, and the tree returns to its place. The surface of the water is smooth. The queen is on her knees before the holy wood. No one has seen the cross, not even Nour, who is fascinated by an unknown place to which the queen has no access—there is more than one path toward truth! Bilqis has come to Solomon to ask for knowledge, and standing here before the holy bridge she finds herself in possession of a knowledge that the king of Israel does not possess: 'Because of this sacred wood the earth shall tremble, the sun and moon shall lose their brightness, the veil of the Temple shall be torn from top to bottom, and many sacred bodies shall be reborn and will be seen in Jerusalem.' Bilqis has barely arrived at the palace, and already a new enigma has been presented to her, one of the keys of the world to come: the annunciation of the martyrdom of a man whom a part of humankind will recognize as their god

"She stands silent and immobile, awed by the sign, rapt to see the strange tree floating again so peacefully in the basin. Her face shows no tension; the queen contains her emotion. She is conscious of having received a new proof of this faculty she cannot control, and against which it is pointless to rebel. She is the depositary of a knowledge that surpasses her, but which does not give her the power to act. She can change nothing in what is to come. The movement of her kneeling body, leaning slightly forward, her head held high, designates the truth. She solemnly acknowledges the tree of life, the wood from Adam upon which the body of 'Jesus, King of the Jews' will be crucified. It is as clear as the inscription pinned to the cross. She cannot walk upon the tree out of respect, because it represents something higher and greater: the passage from one world to another, a passage that humankind is not yet ready to undertake. Her knowledge is a strange one: Her certainty is absolute, but she lacks the words with which to convey it. Facts will speak, and sooner or later; everyone will arrive there, in their own time, at their own pace. Those who resist will get lost along the way. The power of the truth knows no appeal, and it is futile to insist with those who refuse to see. They will not be sensitive to persuasion until they have felt the truth as a certainty themselves. The truth need not make a statement: its silent presence suffices, and anyone who sees it can feel the force of its vision without traversing the hesitation of words. The king is the only one who shall receive the message entrusted to Bilqis: that, too, she knows.

"She continues on her way to the ceremony. And in order not to step on the sacred wood, she steps into the shallow water, lifting the skirt of her robe. She is holding the cloth well above her calves when underneath her feet the consistency of the ground changes. The transparent surface of water is transformed into a pristine crystal. At the same time she is aware of agitation all around her: have others also witnessed the mystery? Women have come to sit along the terraced steps around the basin in the middle of the colorful plants. They whisper, laugh, comment audibly on the way she has strayed from the prescribed path. Their language is not unlike that of Sheba, but sounds more guttural and is difficult to understand—they are talking so quickly! Yet, the mockery in their tone does not escape her. The little maidservant who has been leading them walks behind her. The long white epaulets that adorn her bolero flap with the rapid rhythm of her steps. She steps onto the bridge and tries again to induce the queen to follow her. Bilqis pretends not to see her and makes her way around the wood to the other side. Next to the fountain an elderly woman greets the queen and extends her hand to help her step up out of the basin. The woman's red veil is decorated with blue flowers, and her fore-head is adorned with a simple diadem, accentuating the dignity of her deeply wrinkled face.

"'You are welcome among the women of the court of Solomon—you whose prodigious acts do not protect you from error. You are welcome, for you resemble us. By raising your robe immodestly, by taking the crystal for water in accordance with Solomon's predictions, you have become one of us. We greet you according to the laws of hospitality and forgive you your inappropriate gesture. We are the only ones who saw your ankle; there were no men anywhere nearby.'

"Bilqis is startled—no! She is not like these women who belong to Solomon's harem! She did not mistake the crystal for water, it is the water that suddenly grew hard and changed into crystal. The tree rose out of the water; she saw it, of that she is certain. She must defend herself against such a slanderous accusation. She must refuse to be humiliated or treated as if she were of lower rank. Refusing the outstretched hand, she makes a gesture indicating that she will climb up on the edge on her own. And thenshe hears a sound, a steady note, chanted words. She turns around: Nour is looking toward the place from where the melody comes.The song of Qoum is being chanted by an invisible female voice. The sound carries Bilqis off into another time, another rhythm: What does it matter if, for the moment, she accepts with humility reproaches that are not due her? What does it matter if she is not recognized by these women whom she does not consider to be her equal. Her true dignity lies elsewhere —in the pursuit of her mission. What does it matter if she cannot bring everyone, everywhere and at the same time to recognize the truth—for surely, unveiling the truth is more immodest and unbearable than the unveiling of a woman's calves! Why deny those who do not have the strength to lose the refuge of their pretences? The alliance she has come to conclude with Solomon must not be endangered by petty considerations of pride. She grasps the old woman's hands. With the help of the maidservant with the winged collar, the old woman pulls Bilqis out of the basin.

"'I have wronged myself; I submit, with Solomon, to God, to the Lord of the Worlds.' Bilqis utters these words as if they did not belong to her. Then she hears them: they do not hurt her—on the contrary, they excite her insatiable curiosity. Who is this 'God, Lord of the Worlds,' to whom she has involuntarily pledged her allegiance?"

Chapter nine

Quite suddenly, the evil humors flow abundantly from Silvia body. After a day of total prostration, she is overcome with violent shaking and nausea. Unable to rise from the bed hastily made up for her in an isolated room, she writhes in pain, but also in rage. Around her she hears moans of suffering and useless protests. "Do not struggle so, *Signora!*" There is commotion: a whirlwind of basins, soiled linen,—and the hurried steps of servants who hope to escape as quickly as possible from the pestilence, from excretions of all sorts, from the vision of a body that has lost everything human except the willfulness of its refusal to die, the violence of its struggle against pain, and the defiance of its gaze into the destiny that awaits it. Piero is in the way, hindering their work as they try to change the sheets while he stands by the bed. He does not know where to go, how to behave. In the first hours following their arrival, he sat in silence on a chair by Silvia's bedside and did not move. He showed no reaction to the doctor's air of consternation and contrition as he hastily left the room, or to Marta's devotion as she tried to make Silvia swallow some herbal broth, or to the muffled calm of the maidservants as they prepared to fumigate the bedchamber with pine essence, as if for a holy ritual.

Silvia's sudden agitation makes it impossible to stand by her and gently squeeze her hand or speak of ordinary things. It is also impossible to hold on to the illusion that their worst fears will not come to pass. All through the long hours, Piero has fought off the void with a constant flow of words, insignificant remarks, and he has abstained from pursuing the story of the queen, of conjuring up the image of Bilqis—so alive as she leans gently toward the king of wisdom, her body wrapped in a magnificent white robe in a hall bedecked by golden shields and dominated by a throne encrusted with precious jewels and alabaster. Speaking of her seems incongruous to Piero, an insult to Silvia, trapped in solitude by disease

Faced with the loss of Bilquis' most precious possession, life itself, the notion of wealth has lost all significance. Bilqis was on her way to see Solomon and sought to give her offer of allegiance with perfection. She offered her silence and was eager to exchange ideas, to prove attentive. She was as ready to listen to him as if already in love. But these concerns have become meaningless in the world where Silvia now finds herself, beyond the perception of reality, alone before the great enigma—death—and the essential question—salvation.

Can she still see Piero standing before her? And can she, above all, picture herself—frantic, hair unkempt, blood drained from her face, and these evil humors, unsightly, horrid, as they ooze from her. Dreadful, nauseating, and brownish in color, they gleam and slide over her skin festering with black spots. There is not one inch of her body that is neither sunken nor swollen, strained, or bloated. Silvia—this wise, reserved, serious, devoted, faithful young woman—rebels as she has never done in all her life. She is fighting against the evil that possesses her by every pore in her skin, gripping her and destroying her. She screams and cries out but does not moan; she has become different, worthy of another form of consideration, through this resistance to the demon.

Piero stays by the bed, even though he is shoved about and showered with imperious reprimands: "You must not stay here, *Signore!*" As he stands over her body, invaded by ugliness destroying his wife before his very eyes, he observes, stupefied, the progression of death, and feels contaminated by it. He, too, would like to cry out, to proclaim the horror of his helplessness. He has no remedy with which to counter the hemorrhaging, the diarrhea, the pus and vomiting. And on her disfigured face he can read only pain and suffering:

Silvia no longer has even the refuge of reflection and distance, of her thoughts. No, she is no longer aware of herself. Her body has become nothing but pain; she has no memory of pleasure or well-being, of moments free from suffering, free from the spasms that wring her or the choking that stifles her. With every convulsion that shakes her body, she cries, "No!" In her agitation she knocks over the blackened metal basins the servants bring to her; she pushes away the linen. Now she is naked in the torchlight of the darkened room, and Piero, horrified and fascinated, does not stay solely because Silvia is his wife, but also because he is in thrall to an inadmissible force, a mixture of attraction and repulsion: never before has he so closely experienced both beauty and ugliness, and the disturbing relation between the evil hidden within us all, revealed by illness, and our goodness. Candles and torches cast a reddish light upon her lacerated skin and her twisted limbs, and the image of a splendid force—*how can he even think such a thing!*—evokes, better than anything he knows, the tortures of hell.

Piero with his massive, square build, his body firmly planted upon his strong limbs, his head resolutely turned to face what is before him, suddenly collapses. He can feel a steady, warm flow of tears on his cheeks; something in him is breaking loose, escaping, transforming into a silent cry. The absence of a child, Silvia's illness and her unbearable suffering, the difficulty of loving of devoting oneself to one single object of love amidst the myriad possibilities the world offers... His thoughts flow in a steady stream. His pain breaks apart, dissolves into an immense effusion. At the sight of this huge body, this mass melting and folding upon itself as it stretches out toward the bed, the servants step aside and leave the room. Before he can even put his hand upon Silvia's body, the silent lament of his tears reaches the young woman. The frenzy abates; she is still stretched out and shaking, but no longer thrusts her limbs out in a desperate struggle against the evil gaining on her body. Marta quickly dresses her in a perfectly ironed white shift and covers her with a sheet, on which Piero now lays his forehead. It is soon soaked with his tears. And gradually this moist warmth and the pressure of Piero's forehead, whose weight Silvia has so often felt, bring her back to a certain degree of consciousness. She places her hand on his head and gently caresses his hair in a familiar gesture. He sits up slightly to look at her. Her defiance was frantic, and hopeless. Her eyes, now burning with fever, show her subsiding despair and seem to express acceptance and a peace.

"She is beautiful, our Bilqis...isn't she?"

Piero is not sure he has heard correctly. But he answers, compelled by a semblance of faith.

"Yes, she is beautiful, dignified and serene. She is protected from evil."

"From demons and the spirits that have taken over my body..."

"But against which you are struggling, and resisting. You are right; you are doing what you must. Stay calm now and save your strength."

And in a single breath, before her tormented, ruined body, Piero makes the confession he has withheld since the day of their very first meeting in this same village of Monterchi: "I love you, Silvia, and not only for the harmony you have brought into my life, not only for the anchor you provide for my drifting existence. I love you, Silvia, for yourself, for your gentle beauty, your calm acceptance of life's mysteries, the intelligence with which you read your books, the way you understand Bilqis, and the gift that has enabled you to share her story. I love you, Silvia."

With the pressure of his hand upon her shoulder, Silvia's body relaxes. All her suffering seems to have abated. They raise their heads at the same time: music. Are they sharing a same dream, or has a woman come from another place—from no-where—to sit in the neighboring room to sing and play the harp? Her pure, light voice ascends the scale to sing short phrases enriched with modulations and lively trills, building up to a rapid rhythm.

"Music," murmurs Piero. "Are we already in heaven?"

"It is Bilqis singing," says Silvia.

She searches for a cushion to lean upon. Piero helps her to a steadier position. And the story continues, from the place where she had left it.

"The moment Bilqis knelt before Solomon and placed her hands in the king's, she sensed that he had accepted her tribute, and a slight tremor came over her, a shiver from deep within her body, from the place where one bows and then stands straight again."

With an evocative gesture, Silvia places her hand at the top of her belly, no longer contracting with spasms. Light, fleet-ing tears well again in Piero's eyes. He beholds her with admira-tion and surprise, this woman who has returned from the shores of death to evoke the love between a little queen and a wise prophet.

"The queen lifts her head and, on the verge of trembling, discovers the king's eyes glowing with intelligence and a zest for life above his long white beard. She finds she is confronted with a new enigma, one that demands an even more urgent response than all the difficult questions that have brought her here: What is it that so draws her to this man? Has her perilous voyage not drawn all its significance from this meeting alone? But she is a queen on an official mission, and she must control herself and let nothing show through. A faint smile at the corner of the king's lips shows that he is no fool, and he is very pleased with the effect of his presentation and his charm. Women are a source of great pleasure to him, his most precious wealth—daughters of kings, princesses from faraway lands compete for the honor of charming him. Has it not been said that there are more than a hundred of them living in the women's quarters of his immense palace?

"He is sensitive to the stunning beauty of the new arrival, a beauty based equally on the brilliance of her gaze, her presence, the great subtlety in her use of powders and jewelry and the shape of her face, which is a perfect oval. Her intelligence is also a precious factor; she intrigues him with her ability to surpass him, to proceed quickly and go farther, by countering his threat of a belligerent attack with an embassy she has organized herself. She braved the same deserts her ancestors found so difficult, and she has managed to cross them unharmed; and now she has immediately discovered the mysteries of his palace. At their very first meeting, she told him of the prophecy that was revealed to her in the hall of the precious tree. It speaks of Adam's wood, of a cross on which a man—a king of the Jews of mysterious origins—will be tortured, and of the destruction of the Temple. Solomon feels he has been surpassed and is troubled. Cautiously, without fully understanding the source of such urgency, he orders the destruction of the crystal and the water in which the magnificent tree trunk was embedded, and forbids any mention of the tree, the remains of which are to be buried deep in a ravine. As for Bilqis, once her message has been delivered, she forgets her vision. The image of the cross and the Temple in flames vanishes from within, abandons her. It was as if the vision penetrated her, reached its recipient, then continued on its way toward completion, leaving Bilqis with no memory of it.

"Upon each of his meetings with the queen, Solomon's objections to Sheba—how to convert a new nation, and add yet another people to those who recognize the one God and pay tribute to Israel—all this becomes less urgent, less significant. Solomon envisions another means altogether of attaining his goal. The queen's personality justifies his caution: he has settled her with her ladies-in-waiting in separate quarters from the other women in his household. Bilqis showed no desire to meet them. She even refused their invitation to an afternoon gathering of women where there would be dancing and singing along with sweet beverages and honey pastries. Their mocking and ironic presence around the basin when she arrived at the palace was more than enough. Their desire to absorb her, to make her like them, to welcome her into their community causes her to tremble. How dare they imagine she might give up her position as queen and let herself be reduced to the rank of a concubine!

To a certain degree she has been protected by Ishta's terror, by the anxiety the mother projected on her daughter by forbidding her to use her name because it the echoed the word 'concubine' in her language. Bilqis may have retaken possession of her name, but something intuitive makes her distance herself from any situation involving the risk of submission, anything that might endanger her royal position. How can she be anything other than the sole heir, protected by all and to whom all must bow down?

"That is why envy and jealousy have never touched her. Envy is the business of petty minds, of those who are contented with limited and mediocre possessions and who restrict their power to obtaining immediate gratification of their passions. She has observed the rivalry between her councilors and the tribal chiefs in her entourage, and she has seen what goes on in the women's quarters of her own palace: how quarrels are sparked by trivial matters, how jealousy can flare up, yet it requires little to calm it. This is how Bilqis imagines Solomon's harem: whatever their intelligence or the level of their education, these women are unable to talk in public, among other women, about anything other than those subjects deemed proper for their sex and their status. Bilqis has never had to contend with such rules; even as a small child she has been privy to the mystery of power and the subtleties of religion. It was in the women's quarters at the palace of Sheba that she learned how to enhance her beauty, how to dress and adopt sensitive manners and seductive ways of speaking, of looking, and of moving. But she had never had to compare herself to those around her; nor has she ever been among people who could claim to be her equal or who might threaten her honor. She is prepared, however, to recognize that those grander than herself might actually bring something good to her and to her people, and to the rest of mankind. Thus her tribute to Solomon is sincere: she does not envy him and is convinced that to show honor and respect for a wiser government and a more effective organization of the court in no way detracts from her own power as a queen. His example can only inspire her to new heights of statesmanship and confer her with enhanced majesty, better discernment, and wiser judgment.

"For three days, in the midafternoon, Solomon calls Bilqis to one of the reception halls of his palace. She tests him with the hard questions she has prepared, and he replies cautiously, placing before her one by one, as he unfolds them, the petals that protect the heart of those flowers that are understanding and intelligence. He discovers multiple meanings, preserving mystery all the while, as well as the possibility of other interpretations. She listens, follows his words, and derives an intense satisfaction from inferring things that, full of meaning, remain hidden yet avoid any complete revelation. She trembles, too, with other sensations: the moment she sees Solomon before her, seated on his throne at the top of the platform at the end of the succession of doors opening before her, the rhythm of her breathing changes, the palms of her hand become moist, and something thrilling draws her to him as a shiver runs through her body. She recognizes the signs that echo in the hushed voices of women when they speak of love.

"Solomon feels equally troubled. The desire she arouses in him is calm and deep, without urgency. It is rooted in a harmony of the senses and an intelligence that he has found in no other woman. When she questions him on his army, his chariots, or the way he ensures the loyalty of his generals, he chisels his answers, making them so sharp that he manages to attain an unprecedented degree of precision. She knows how to ask the right questions and accept answers only when they have reached their most clarified state. Solomon, too, feels something stirring him in her presence, but he stays his hand from touching hers. He observes her, watching as her fingers point toward the sky to designate the heights that her celestial questions probe. For Solomon this is a delicious combat: to stimulate his mind, he must restrain his desire.

"He likes the resistance this woman puts up to the simplest of offers, her insistence on showing that she is never what she appears to be. He smiles as she tries to keep a distance that others would consider haughtiness, and he grants her the privilege of an apartment separate from the other women. He fears nothing; he knows already that he has won. By accepting and acknowledging as a fault what she knows is really the effect of the charms he has at his disposal, she has demonstrated her allegiance to him. She has made amends for an error she did not commit. She has understood that what was revealed to her must remain hidden—that the water she saw, and felt, must remain, for everyone else, a crystal mirror. He admires her determination and the intelligence of her diplomacy, her judicious evaluation of objectives. She concedes one victory to him in order to obtain another, to attain a knowledge of government, religion, and the meaning of life that she has come to him to find. She has renounced brilliance for the time being, and allows him to appear to be the victor so as to enable her to obtain the favors expected of her embassy.

"After three days have gone by, Solomon decides to go to her unannounced, along the secret corridor. It runs alongside the apartments where she is staying, and enables him to see without being seen. The siesta time has passed; he does not want to surprise her while she is in a vulnerable state of drowsiness. He wants to receive that vulnerability like a gift, at a time of his choosing. But he enjoys disconcerting her: he cancelled their afternoon meeting without explanation, for he was curious to see how she would spend that time in this unfamiliar place, liberated from all the duties of her reign and from any business in his presence.

"Solomon walks along the corridor that has been hollowed out between the two walls. When he reaches the vicinity of Bilqis' apartments, his attention is caught by a gentle, quiet sound, like flowing water. He stands looking through a horizontal chink in the wall, an opening made opaque with alabaster, which from the other side looks like nothing more than a line between two rows of stone. It takes him a moment to adjust his gaze and see the entire room. Bilqis is seated at the foot of the bed on a bench of supple woven reed with a high wooden back planted firmly on rectangular feet. She has left her hair loose, pulled back over her shoulders. She is wearing large silver earrings with multiple pendants, a mixture of finely wrought gold pieces and bright jewels mounted on woven silver threads. Her gown is simple and flowing as an indoor garment should be. It is woven in a fine white canvas and embroidered with golden thread. As she sits, the gown flows around her. She has gathered the folds in her lap to form a sort of cushion, on which a small harp rests. The way she has carefully placed her feet upon a wooden stool shows that she is a practitioner who is attentive to the proper position of the instrument. Her light garment falls from her shoulders and follows the flowing movement of her arms around the instrument, down to her hands, where her fingers pluck the strings in a harmonious movement. Solomon admires the musician's delicate wrists, the supple movement of her fingers. The contrast between the sinuous movement of her arms, hands, and fingers, and the majestic bearing of her head, her firm straight body upon the rigid seat, makes a deep impression upon the king: this woman is made for the sweetness of love as much as for the rigors of power.

"Frozen in contemplation and mesmerized by the flowing sounds of the melody, Solomon does not hear her singing at first, so subtle is the fusion between the instrument and her voice. Her pronunciation eliminates the guttural sounds, but he recognizes the text: the poem that his father David composed when he was in the desert of Judah:

"*O God, thou art my God; early will I seek Thee: my soul thirsteth for Thee.*

"Moved, rapt, Solomon is led to a world that is different from his own. The young woman's interpretation fills the words she has borrowed from David with a new sensibility, a new sensuality. She sings the psalm without denying her identity as a woman from the high desert plateaus. Using minute pauses and unexpected high notes at the end of each phrase, Bilqis introduces a stranger's questioning, emblematic of her curious gaze that she trains upon the world: *To which God is she speaking? What is she looking for? To whom is she promising her love? To whom does she affirm:* 'To see thy power and thy glory, so as I have seen Thee in the sanctuary.'?

"Her fervor betrays desire, and Solomon hardly dares to admit to himself that he wishes to be as much the object of that desire as God is. Is she leading him to blasphemy? And yet nevertheless, the music has a purity about it, an authenticity that brings it closer to voices from above, the messenger of another knowledge.

"*My soul followeth hard after Thee: Thy right hand upholdeth me.*'

"Solomon shivers, takes his eyes from the chink, and leans against the wall just behind him. At the end of the psalm, the voice stops. Solomon remains motionless, hesitating between action and flight, and postpones all the projects that have been utterly changed by this interruption of the sacred and the psalm: the strangeness of this woman's power awes him. He is no longer watching her, he cannot see her, and all of a sudden he can smell her perfume and sense her presence in the narrow

corridor only a few steps away: She has discovered the hidden
entrance, the passage between the room and the corridor. She is
walking toward him with her hand outstretched, and he takes it,
despite everything that is customary."

Silvia's story was interrupted only by a few coughing fits. Nothing else in her clear speech displayed evidence of the illness destroying her.

Her body is again as white as the sheets and the shift in
which she is clothed. She has paused, somewhat out of breath.
All through her story her eyes remained fixed on the beams
above the bed as if the words have come to her from above. Just
as Solomon is preparing to follow the queen into her room, Silvia turns to Piero, and in the burning anguish in her eyes, he
can see everything at once: fever, desire, the disease consuming
her, the raging of the senses, and the intensity that transforms
her—all are conveyed, they imprint a profound change upon
the atmosphere of the room, which has been temporarily abandoned by the servants.

Piero's hand trembles, but he raises it toward her waiting
face, her parted lips, and then down to her neck; his gentle fingers hardly touch her skin. In turn, Silvia's hand reaches toward
Piero's face, then comes to rest on his other arm as he leans over
her. She moves her hand from his wrist to his forearm, gently,
slipping it beneath the cloth of his sleeve with its starched pleats.
"Did you know that it was for the love of the Queen of Sheba
that Solomon became a poet?"

"I only know what you have told me," murmurs Piero.

"Then listen, my beloved, to the song which the king
composed for the queen, the present the queen received from
the king:

*"My beloved is mine, and I am his: he feedeth among the lil-
ies.*

*Until the daybreak, and the shadows flee away, turn, my be-
loved,*

*and be thou like a roe or a young hart upon the mountains
of Bether.*

Piero lies down on the bed, mindful not to crush her: she
is so fragile. Their bodies now side by side, she relaxes against
him, and their slow, gentle caresses lead them into sleep. When
Marta comes back to the room, she stops short on the threshold:
how carelessly this couple lies intertwined, when the plague is
abroad, and one of them has already succumbed to it! Silvia
tosses, and begins to moan. A new fit is approaching.

"*Signore, Signore!*" cries Marta, gently shaking Piero.
"Come *Signore,* you must leave her now."

Dazed, Piero rises without speaking, and grabs hold of
the indoor cloak he had tossed on the bed. Marta leads him
away, quickly, before the convulsions begin again.

"Go and pray, *Signore.* Go to the chapel, the Virgin will
help us. Go and pray, that's the most useful thing you can do.
And here I'll do what God gives me the power to accomplish."

Chapter ten

Every moment counts in Monterchi, while in the calm succession of days at Solomon's palace, there is no sign to suggest that someday everything might possibly come to an end. On the morning after her first night with the king, the young queen found the jewels that Nour had laid out for her on her dressing table: the coral necklace with the single, inlaid pearl. She had chosen it herself, in Sheba, from among the many jewels that her chest contained, to celebrate her meeting with her beloved. At that time she had imagined him to be young, with black eyes and thick curls. Now she laughs as she thinks of the man, his beard already white, who was at her side when she awoke. He has enabled her to experience her sensations to the fullest, something she had only the faintest hint of when the more daring of her maidservants would caress her. This broad-shouldered man with his ample body, his agile hands, and soft words, now occupies all her thoughts. A sort of murmur hums within her in the constant repetition of his name. These sensations give reality to her dreams at last.

While Nour is fastening the light coral necklace around her bare neck, she laughs from the gentle ripples of a pleasure she can still feel; she laughs upon seeing how rosy her cheeks are—and yet she has not yet used any powders. She laughs at her breasts as she observes them lift in the mirror, as if sculpted by firm, knowing hands; she smiles to see the fresh, childlike air on her face once again, a look that had disappeared behind the mask of royalty and responsibility, decision making and law enforcement, and the difficult journey homeward that awaits her. Her forehead is smooth again, she no longer clenches her jaw, and in her eyes she can see delight and joy, gaiety and lightness, and the peace that comes of being sure at last: He has arrived, the man who will fulfill her most secret desires and give her the keys to the world—and this shall last, day after day, without fear of the morning, a morning which will arrive in the continuity of a perfect night. At sunrise, she sits at her dressing table and laughs as she recalls the words that Solomon murmured into her ear:

> *How beautiful are thy feet with shoes, O prince's daughter!*
> *The joints of thy thighs are like jewels, the work of the hands*
>   *of a cunning workman.*
> *Thy navel is like a round goblet, which wanteth not liquor:*
> *Thy belly is like a heap of wheat set about with lilies.*
> *Thy two breasts are like two young roes that are twins...*

As the weeks go by, she loves as she learns, learns as she loves She consults the priests and men of law and even the general of the army; she reads the scrolls in the library and the sacred texts. Nour follows her from daybreak until the late hours, when she joins Solomon as he tends to the affairs of his kingdom. Nour does not seek to temper the queen's juvenile enthusiasm, nor to remind her that no love is simple, above all for a queen. Yet in the poems that Bilqis recites to her in the morning, Nour notices how persistently Solomon evokes the sixty queens and eighty concubines that are the glory of his palace: as for Bilqis, she only delights in the unique experience of being the perfect, chosen favorite.

Nour remains watchful: Such a long absence is not without risk to the unity of the kingdom beyond the desert, left without a ruler. Messengers from Sheba are rare, and for the moment there is no cause for alarm. Those who have accompanied the queen have been richly welcomed by Solomon's entourage, each according to his rank. They send enthusiastic tales to the tribes of the land of incense, and all expect to benefit greatly from this journey. Nour remains confident: urgency will restore Bilqis to her duties; even love cannot cause her to forget them.

Nour often stands in the little courtyard overlooked by all the rooms of their apartment. This square space, dazzling with light, looks uncannily like the queen's refuge in her own palace. The texture of the walls is different, an apparent limestone that is granular and cut into regular parallelepipeds. This stone absorbs the rays of light and attenuates the dazzling, blinding sensation. The fountain at the center is decorated with an identical sculpture to her one at home: a woman whose arm is raised to celebrate the restoration, through flowing water, of purity to life. The hoopoe has returned to perch on the fountain's edge and seems to share lengthy consultations with Nour regarding the future the queen is making for herself.

Bilqis often passes through here. She waits for Solomon as evening falls, and it is pleasant to sit on the edge of the fountain. The silvery chime of the water sliding over stone suffices to procure an impression of coolness, and Bilqis reproduces the gestures which, in Sheba, gave her serenity: she dips her hands into the water, then raises in a bowl toward her lowered face as she lets the water flow through her open fingers. Nothing arouses in her either the astonishment, the memory, or even the evocation of another place. She contemplates the flame tree, looks with the same eagerness as in Sheba at its gleaming clusters of blossoms, but she is not surprised to see it planted here in the same place as in the courtyard of her faraway palace: She feels here as if she were there. She asks herself no questions and forgets the exceptional nature of these circumstances. She is in love and nothing surprises her. She has faith in the king's ability to accomplish miracles, to be obeyed beyond space, to draw time out.

In Monterchi, Piero obeys Marta's orders. He leaves the house. Silvia is now facing another crisis in her struggle against the disease, but though he feels torn, he also feels useless and in the way. He knows that by going to Santa Maria di Momentana, he will not feel like he is betraying or abandoning her: he will be able to remember her as she was in the freshness and spontaneity of their first encounter.

Piero takes a horse and slowly makes his way down the somewhat steep slope that leads to the banks of the Cerfone. The ford seems easier to cross here than on the other side of the hill, where they arrived, by the Borgo road. In two days the water level has dropped considerably. How quickly nature changes, moving for no apparent reason from anger to kindness toward mankind! The temperature has risen, the sun is shining high in the sky, and the light sharpens the shapes of things with great clarity. At the river's edge, a brilliant yellow shrub lends a festive touch to the cluster of trees and the bushes poised between drab winter's gray and the budding green of springtime. Does this sign of renewal bode well for Silvia's illness? Piero would like to believe so, he hopes the future will not be made of mourning and pain.

Piero reins in his horse. By the river, where planks have been roughly assembled to make a small platform to ease access to the shore, he bends down to touch the ground: What was the queen's field of vision when she knelt down before the sacred wood? He cannot imagine the scene as Silvia described it. The fallen tree serves as a bridge across a vast indoor pool? The enchantments of the Orient are too distant for Piero. He does not deny them, but they belong to Silvia. His vision is different, closer to the reality they experienced together when Silvia, seated exhausted by the river's edge, suddenly broke her silence to pick up the thread of her story.

Now he returns to the path toward the chapel, where a surprise awaits him: the fountain is gone. Or rather, he sees that there never was a fountain there. He must face the facts: The small wall surrounding the source of water is too old; it must have always been in this place. It was into a very ordinary well, massive and unadorned, that Silvia must have leaned to bring up her bucket of water and splash and refresh herself after her work in the church. And yet what had firmly taken hold in Piero's memory was the image of an elegant fountain, sur-mounted by a statue. He thought that upon returning here he would find the exact fountain of his memory—and now to the contrary, he must resign himself to the fact that it never existed. He is troubled by such a failure of memory, such confusion. The mathematical rigor of his mind is shaken. Who can he trust if he doubts even his own judgment?

In the little chapel, nothing has changed. The light enters sparingly through the only window, and the nave is still bathed in a gentle darkness. He does not linger by the altar against the left-hand wall, in front of the wooden sculpture of Virgin and Child—the object of his grandmother's devotion. The ugliness of the painting above the central altar, another Virgin and Child surrounded by two angels, horrifies him as much as it always has. He can bear the old-fashioned use of gilt less than ever, and the awkwardness of heavily outlined features, a composition that fails to take into account the most elementary laws of measuring or the ratio of proportion between objects based on the distance that separates them from the spot from where they are viewed.

The presence of a painting like this is all the more un-bearable in this place where his salvation was won, where the Virgin granted the prayers of his grandmother and where he saw Silvia for the first time. He must fulfill his vow at last! He does not share the materialist, accountable conception of religion to which some profess; the acts of God are not the mirror image of our own, for otherwise He would not be God. God does not keep a petty ledger of our promises or our penances, he does not measure His good deeds or graces according to the measure of our constant pettiness, and he will not refuse to answer Piero's prayer if Piero does not fulfill the commitment he made in his youth. Painting, however, is the only way for him to establish a connection with the heavens, to put to good use the gifts given him, to do use that which God, in this very place, granted him—the use of his hands; that is the most effective of prayers.

Standing before the altar, the words fail to come to his lips, to invoke, according to custom, the protection of the mother of God. He merely murmurs Silvia's name, addressing it to the woman who has always protected him, imagining the work he will undertake. He will keep the same figures—the Virgin and two angels—but he will change the style completely, as well as the use of space, and he will offer a totally different vision of the child. The actual painting above the altar begins to fade; he no longer sees it. He is seeking to bring his Virgin to life, to imagine the features he will give her—he who is incapable of working without a model. He listens to his subject; he questions this woman who was closest to God by giving birth to his son: What does she have to say to him, a man who has been incapable of fathering a child. A phrase comes to mind at that moment, in the haven of the little chapel, as if it Mary's were answering his plea:

"Take whatever comes as a good deed."

Then he hears a second sentence, another line from the hymn by Saint Francis that Silvia quoted to him on their first meeting: "All praise be yours, my Lord, through Sister Death, from whose embrace no mortal can escape." Death is a law as ancient as the first man. In the mouth of the first dead man, Adam, the seed of the tree of the Cross, the new covenant between God and mankind, was planted., One must obey the laws of death. Piero's eyes fill with tears—he who never cries! And now twice in the same day. Through his tears he manages to utter the words that lead him to the place he would prefer not to go: "Yes, I consent, but in suffering and difficulty. I consent because I have faith in the promise of resurrection and paradise. In that heavenly garden, the angels will guide me to the tent for rest, where Silvia will be waiting for me, like the queen, in the desert, waited for Solomon."

Moriah, a name moist with sweetness… Bilqis learns it from Solomon on the day he takes her for the first time to the Temple. *Moriah…* Each syllable rings out like the annunciation of a deliverance. *Moriah…*It was in this place that tradition places the sacrifice of Abraham; it was here that David chose to build the Temple and that Solomon accomplished what his father desired. *Moriah…*where the hand of the angel seized the father's arm the moment he was preparing to slit the child's throat. The infernal spiral of the gods' demand for victims had been broken.

At the heart of the Temple, where no women are allowed, the priests give honor to the Ark of the Covenant entered into between a God and his people. Under the signs of a spared human life, and of a father who was restored to the power of life over his child and was able to spare him from evil. The ceremony of the pascal lamb commemorates this event, and in the Temple, Solomon increases the number of the blood sacrifices, letting the animals' blood according to a very elaborate ritual worthy of his God's attention and likely to elicit, once again, his mercy. The nightmare that had haunted Bilqis' sleep after her father's death has been transformed into a gentle reality: when she awakes, a man's arm is encircling her neck, but it is not to threaten her with the blade of sacrifice. On the contrary, Solomon's arm protects her, it wards off all threats, and she surrenders, placing her trust in the king, and the god he honors on the hill of Moriah.

Bilqis gladly allows herself to be led through the halls of the Temple; she grows giddy with the gentle poignancy and joyous vigor of the music, the heady charm or unctuous aroma of the perfumes, the brightly colored cloths and munificence of the bronze wall, the wood carvings, the splendid ivories and the thick beams of precious wood. She agrees to be purified with holy water according to the rites established for visitors, and to kneel down and present offerings—as they do in Sheba for Almaqah. But now she will feel no anxiety or fear of the consequences that might befall her or her people with any error she might make. Since Yahweh, the God of Abraham, stayed the hand of Abraham, he cannot take offence at a ritual not carried out exactly according to the rules. In everything she sees and hears, she selects certain sensations and details in order to construct her own point of view, bit by bit—her own thoughts, her own history. She has not forgotten the secret purpose of this journey: to find the answers to her questions, to learn to be a better ruler, and to discover the key to power and the way to exercise it with wisdom rather than force. What does it matter if her interpretation of Abraham's sacrifice does not conform to that of the priests! Surely no one will take offence at the failings of a foreigner, especially not Solomon, who loves her and understands her.

Her visit to the Temple has elated her, and she surrenders to the many inner resonances inspired by the name of Moriah. When she returns to the room in the palace and sits at the table that has been opulently decorated by the maidservants, she prepares to share her impressions with Solomon, to let him to share in her joy and enthusiasm, and thus she begins to evoke the sacrifice of Abraham. But Solomon interrupts her and does not let her speak. In a sententious voice he comments upon the story of the founding sacrifice. He evokes neither mercy nor kindness; he insists on emphasizing Abraham's absolute obedience to his god, and Isaac's submission to the incomprehensible demands of his father.

"Thus," he adds, "all men must comply, blindly, with the commands of the one God and his representative on earth, the King of Israel. All people must honor Yahweh without reservation and submit to the laws of the government He has chosen so that His all powerful will, be done."

Bilqis does not recognize the man standing before her— his closed face, his body rigid as though he is wearing armor. This is not the lover speaking to the woman he loves, the ma-

ture man who delights in opening horizons to his young companion. This is an absolute monarch proclaiming a sentence,
tolerating neither discussion nor distortion; a conquering king,
who threatens those who offer the slightest form of resistance,
and a man of power who allows only the most submissive
courtiers to enter his entourage. His attitude has suddenly become hostile, and his gaze is imperative and inaccessible to any
form of understanding. He gives orders and demands obedience. He erects a wall between them.

Bilqis shivers, but resists. Something in her refuses to ab-
dicate—it is out of the question for her to forget the dignity of
her people or her position as queen! Her father's legacy is there
to remind her: it has come between hers and the king, who
would impose an untenable suzerainty over her.

But she does not yet need to say "no," to take that risk
and refuse the alliance. Solomon is already talking about something else, commenting on the arrangement of their dinner table, the multitude of small dishes filled with varied succulent
foods; sweet and spicy mixtures of surprising and exquisite sa-
vors and textures. In his constant concern for perfection, he
demands that the harmony of colors match that of tastes, and
that each dish on the table should contribute to a colorful yet
ordered tapestry. Once again he corrects the errors, moves one
plate further to the right, switches the place of two others, asks
for Bilqis' advice regarding the juxtaposition of the straw-
colored yellow of a chickpea paste and the bright red peppers in
the neighboring bowl. Bilqis still feels troubled by the change in
Solomon's attitude: this will to power that has suddenly encom-
passed everything, annihilating any possibility for dialogue,
transforming their relation. She is upset, and her emotion is
visible on her face: her jaws are hollowed, a few lines crease her
brow, and tears are welling at the corner of her eyes. Solomon
notices nothing—he does not see her! He is joking again, his
glances full of a teasing desire as he takes her hand with a loving
tug and guides it toward the plates.

Startled, she realizes that Solomon sees in others only the reflection of himself! Other people interest him only as the mirror of his own desires. He expects Bilqis to reflect the words, the gestures, and the attitudes that stir his senses and his intelligence. But what she feels independently of him, everything that is removed from his own sphere of experience is that a matter of indifference to him? He ignores her, and if she obligated him to show concern for her, he would see this as troublesome, an obstacle to his own pleasure. He would react with anger, impatience, and deep disappointment. He cannot imagine that anyone by his side might dare not to feel, think, and react exactly the way he expects. That is the limit of his understanding and his ability to perceive the reality hidden behind appearances.

The strength and certainty of his judgment are at the basis of his reputation in the exercise of justice and power. It enables him to command all men—and women—for the fulfillment of his desires. At times his faculties seem to wander, they are weakened or obscured by his assurance and self-confidence—equally precious assets for the exercise of power, but which, in excess, may compromise the fragile equilibrium on which his power is based. He is too sure of himself and no longer takes the trouble to consider others; he is deceived by his will to see them conform in every way to his own desires. He has chosen Bilqis for her exceptional personality, for her discernment so like his own, but he is so sure of his victory in the sparring of seduction and intelligence between them that he forgets the woman, and the queen, and he sees only the submissive courtesan, no different from all the other king's daughters who make up his harem.

Bilqis observes him, although he has lost sight of her. It makes her dizzy: in one instant she can see both the danger and the way to ward off the danger, Solomon's strong will and his weaknesses. He can wait no more: He comes to her, embraces her. The meal will be for later, she succumbs to his caresses. She feels his hands, his lips—the strength of his desire. It is not just a physical desire at work, this feeling that draws him to her. He loves her, she has no doubt of that. He loves her in the way a powerful man is able to love. And for her part, the legacy of her father requires her to love him in the way a powerful woman is permitted to love, with the limits such a power imposes. She surrenders, knowing all the while that at any given moment, she will have to invoke that other form of power, that which love gives her over the king, in order to negotiate freedom for her and her people. Pleasure, joy, and warm vibrant sensations have taken possession of her, but all naiveté has vanished with the illusion of an impossible recklessness and the certainty of the end. She feels a pang of regret, regret for the childlike enthusiasm that has born her aloft for these few weeks; at the same time, she is once again fully herself: a queen and a woman—a woman in love, and a proud queen. The violence of her pleasure compels Solomon to look at her: "Thou art fair, Bilqis, fair as the moon, clear as the sun, and terrible as an army with banners."

Piero is unable to leave the chapel behind, to return to the terror-filled reality awaiting him in the village. Fear immediately followed upon his consent: to consent to the death of another is also to consent to one's own death! He seeks comfort in the thoughts of his mother. She had refused to go with them and stayed behind in Borgo: "What do you think the plague can do to my poor body!" was her answer to his pleas. "In any case, in your father's absence nothing will make me leave our house. You must protect Silvia, that is all that matters. I will gladly give you Monterchi for your shelter and Marta's care. On the road, beware of the spirits of the forest. I've always dreaded the dangers hidden in the forest undergrowth—there are devils lurking in the shadows. I shall pray for you."

Where did her prayers go astray, leaving misfortune to assail them so? In the forest, Piero has never felt any fear. Instinctively, he flees from darkness; he refuses to confront it. Wherever the forest is at its thickest and the growth is most dense, he finds a gap, a way through, offered to the golden powder cast by beams of light. And it is light that is of interest to him at the heart of obscurity, it is the mystery he must seize between the grains of pigments. Shadow is only threatening when it is infrangibly thick, as at the heart of the night when the voyager's lamp is extinguished and blackness melts everything into an indistinct mass. At this point there is nothing more that one's gaze—or a painting—can do. But as long as there is still a hope of regaining clarity, all is not lost! No, obscurity has nothing to do with the disaster that has befallen them: they brought death along with them from the town where his mother stayed behind and are in greater danger now than in the depths of the forest. Demons, genies, and gnomes only exist in a world not graced by light, not like the world Silvia finds in the Orient of the Queen of Sheba or the world as depicted by the other women he loves and respects: his mother and Marta. His is a mind concerned with science, eager to discover— thanks to the use of perspective in painting—the hidden structure behind apparent reality cannot be troubled by mysterious, occult, hidden presences.

In the absence of candlelight the chapel remains plunged in gloom, but suddenly a golden arrow from the sky penetrates the glass of the sole opening above the portico. The beam of light falls obliquely toward the center of the retable, where the Virgin's face appears: it is Silvia's face, expressing both the serenity of waiting and the pain of knowing. At the same time, Piero again hears the music of the woman's voice that had sounded so pure to his ears, and to Silvia's just before she awoke, overcoming her illness so that she might continue her story: "It is the voice of Bilqis," she murmurs in Piero's memory.

Such moments, still so recent, are already a memory, obliterated by the next crisis, which may be fatal. Silvia will become a memory: the thought of this terrifies him, angers him. What is the point of his strength, his ability to move scaffolds, carriages caught in the mud, or trees fallen across the path, if he is powerless against death? What is the point of his talent as a painter—his ability to depict a reality close to one's gaze, to honor the commissions of princes and monasteries—if he cannot preserve life? The music is still there, humming insistently in his ear. It is a fragile voice reaching for the sky with confidence, a melody whose modulations waver between lament and tenderness. Where is it coming from? Mathematics can provide no answer. And yet he hears it! Where does this image on the wall, illuminated by sunlight, come from? Gradually it fades until the other Virgin with her clumsy, expressionless face, the only one who actually exists in this place, reappears.

Death is still there, an ineluctable prospect: the whirlwind of the plague has taken Silvia away from him. No miracle was sprung from his prayer—on the contrary, it has shown him the path of acceptance. But he hears the music, the light has come to him, and the painting has taken shape. With the confirmation of death has come the means to struggle against disappearance: he must exhibit memory through painting, not in its tangible precision—after all, it was his own memory that transformed a sturdy well into an elegant fountain—but through the transposition of reality into another dimension, where beauty joins with infinity, where the quest for truth accepts the presence of the invisible, the unknown, the enigmatic, in a splendor of blueness capturing, softening the light.

Bilqis can hear the clamor all the way to the little courtyard, a sound that scales the high walls surrounding her after its passage along the endless corridors and halls of the palace. "Long live Solomon! May the name of Yahweh be eternally associated with the Temple which our king has built."

Her eyes fill with tears of emotion: she sees herself back in Sheba, as a sovereign, as if in Solomon's palace by the window in the throne room—celebrated, adulated, carried by the fervor and ardor, the unanimous approval of the court and of her people. She misses the cheers of the crowd. How she has changed! How far she has come from the little queen who stood in a courtyard not unlike this one to flee from the shouts of her councilors when they sought to praise her after her victory: the tears that ran down her cheeks then were not tears of pleasure, but of fear at the prospect of assuming the power her father had bequeathed her, fear, too, of the gifts of discernment and conviction the gods had bestowed upon her. She had trembled after she had been called on to mete out justice, after she had rallied all the tribes to her plan to set out on an embassy to Jerusalem. She had been afraid of herself, she had felt the need to flee from herself. Today, she envies the king. Not once since she arrived in Jerusalem has she received tributes from the crowd. She refused to take second place, so that place has now been awarded to the new concubine from the land of Edom. How could she, Bilqis, Queen of Sheba, have gone out onto the square at Solomon's side to hear the ovations addressed to the king of Israel alone: He is the one the crowd is cheering and gazing at. He is the one who receives all their enthusiastic attention. She deserves to be the one who, alone, is the subject of the people's cheers.

Solomon the Mighty is honored in the name of Yahweh, and at his side is a new bride for whom he has made sacrifices to foreign gods. In Jerusalem, as in Sheba, men slip into the crowd to encourage the people to voice the required cheers, vital for the king's propaganda. How can Solomon dare to invoke the name of Yahweh when he has so gravely disobeyed him?

When she had dared to comment upon his behavior, the king's response was brutal.

"Who are you to reproach me with disobeying the commands of my god! What do you know of our laws and our commandments?"

"I know what your priests have taught me."

"You were born in impiety, and yet after only a few weeks spent studying our scripture, you lay claim to the words of the righteous! What do you know of the best way to contribute to the glory of Yahweh? Is it a greater sin to place a few offerings upon the altar of the gods of Edom in order to win a new ally and avoid a conflict, than to persist in a futile rigor that could endanger peace and prosperity? From the beginning of my reign, our people have been free from war and have been able to devote themselves entirely to the service of the god whose name has at last been received in the heart of the Temple. Without the peace and the ties I have established with other peoples, I would never have been able to amass such quantities of gold and wood to carry out the task with which Yahweh entrusted me: to complete the lavish, magnificent house my father David had decided to build to celebrate His glory."

With these words Solomon justified his double betrayal to Bilqis—he had betrayed their love, and he had betrayed his god—on the evening when she reproached him with bitter words for the unholy tribute he had agreed to pay to the gods of his fiancée. As for his new marriage—he had not even had the courage to inform her of it himself.

That was only two days ago, and already the new wife had moved into the palace, following the offering of a blood sacrifice on the altar of her gods, and Solomon is using the voice of his people to suggest that this irreverent act never even took place! Solomon proves to be as clever in the art of compromise as in the solving of hard questions. What then is man, if he who is considered to be the wisest among them compromises the facts—and his god, and his women—and plays with reality at the expense of the truth? What is the exercise of power if it forces people to act and think in accordance with the king's own desires, in the name of political imperatives of which he has made himself the sole judge rather than guide one's people toward good?? What reason is there for diplomacy, if it leads to such subterfuge and distortion an atmosphere of ignorance, and the denial of love, the most natural and sacred of laws!

"Love! You women speak of nothing else, and you distort it for your own purposes. You claim that the ties of love must be close and exclusive, but love is a joy that must be exhibited on the scale of the universe! And if you loved me as you claim to do, you would be happy to become part of my plans. You would see it as an honor, not a humiliation. You would perceive that within your blindness you refuse to see: the importance for our two nations of this alliance with Edom, which controls the passage of the caravans between Aqaba and Gaza, the only route over land between Sheba and Jerusalem. I suggest you stay by my side, take part in the edification of a kingdom worthy of Yahweh's greatness, whom you say I am neglecting. You consider the dignity of your people has been affected because you think you have been abandoned! But I shall only abandon you for a few evenings, a few nights. I will return to you often!"

At this point in his speech, Solomon turned to her with a gaze full of desire, as powerful as during the first days and just as full of promise for pleasure and sensual delights. He turned his hand towards her, his palm to the sky, to solicit her alliance once again, but he did not insist: he did not want her to obey, but to come to him of her own volition. He wanted her to adopt his point of view without reservation or reticence. Bilqis was profoundly troubled by this situation. She still felt a powerful attraction to him, yet the moment he imposed on her such an equivocal choice, she resented him for filling her with uncertainty about her own judgments and what she must do. The image of her father came to her at that moment, of circumstances when he, too, had confronted her with such a compromise. There were times when he would take her to his private study to simply partake as a witness in his secret meetings with his enemies. He sought to show by example how to twist facts in his favor, to toy with reality to transform the victim into the executioner. He demonstrated how to simulate total ignorance of the circumstances to determine his interlocutor's point of view, to treat him as an equal in order to flatter him, to make him feel at ease and then use against him that which was revealed in confidence. She despised her father for compromising her through this show of sincerity. Who could one trust if one's own father proved to be capable of the worst perfidy? In such moments she felt close to her mother, victim as she had been of a plot, of betrayal—in the name of power—by the being closest to one's heart—father, husband, lover, friend. How right Ishta had been to teach her wariness, in her fears that her daughter might be reduced to the rank of a simple concubine. If the world is so ugly, if power so easily flouts justice and truth in the name of obscure imperatives, how can one keep from sinking into distress and anger and a surfeit of despair?

The little courtyard has always been her refuge. Today, it is here that she waits for the end of Solomon's nuptials with the little princess from Edom. The cheers of the people of Israel ring out for her as a call from the people of Sheba. And for the first time since she arrived in Jerusalem, Bilqis has noticed the similarity between the sunny courtyard contiguous to her apartments and the square sun-washed space hidden between the two thick walls in her palace in Sheba. The ruby-colored tree, the fountain, the high white walls...Everything is the exact replica of her secret hideaway. To help her forget the distance and avoid nostalgia, Solomon, thanks to the power of his enchantments, did not hesitate to reconstruct the places that were dearest to her. But charm can also have the opposite effect: the familiarity of a place and the absence of strangeness can facilitate the passage from one state to another, from one time to another, from anger to appeasement, from wounded pride and scorned love to a calm decision of departure and acceptance. What she has experienced here is only one moment, a passage whose consequences will be played out there, in Sheba...

Bilqis drifts into a sort of vagueness, and any inclination she might have had to resist seems to have vanished. She is neither torn nor hurt by the prospect of departure, but merely slips into continuity. After the emotion and agitation of anger, then the exaltation she felt on hearing the cheering of the crowd, a sort of languor has come over her. She sits on a stone bench by the flame tree in the shadow of the wall. She feels the heat not only around her, but welling up through every pore in her body. She feels heavy and weighty, and she submits to the soothing sound of water trickling gently from the fountain. She has entered into a strange place, an "in between," "not yet there," and "no longer really here," a space that belongs only to her, with no exact location, as vague as this place itself—she cannot say whether it enchants her in its own sake or because of all the memories it contains. The clarity and rigor, far too demanding, have been stifling her, but now seem to be gently loosening their grip. In asking for too much clarity she has angered Solomon and endangered future relations between Israel and Sheba. Displaying some uncertainty regarding her decisions and desires will help her to obtain more from the king than he would care to give; he is utterly absorbed by the young Edomite who has just arrived at the court. It will not be difficult to negotiate her departure: her presence has become a burden and, in the end, it is of little importance.

From the edge of the fountain, the hoopoe cries out, *oop! oop!* and then, with cumbersome strokes, lifts into the air, spreading its colorful wings. It circles round the little courtyard twice, then flies away.

"Israel's time for the hoopoe is over," says Nour, watching as the bird heads off to the west.

"And for you?" asks the queen; she knows her lady-in-waiting well enough now to infer what she is trying to say through her external examples.

"Here I have found love and, no doubt, the land of my origins. You, too, will know how to find, among your ancestors, a love worthy of you."

The queen reaches out her hand to Nour, a sign that she approves of her choices and that she is granting her liberty. She stays on alone in the little courtyard, observing the fountain and its statue, which suddenly seem very ordinary to her. Without the hoopoe, it has lost all its charm. The flame tree, bursting with life, also urges her to depart.

Despite discretion, The queen senses a newcomer's arrival to this enclosed space. Despite his attempt at discretion, the man's presence becomes known the moment he enters. She recognizes the gardener from her childhood, the one who had come from the same faraway lands as her mother. He bows slightly before her, then goes over to the flame tree to prune it of the branches that have lost their blossoms.

Piero heads slowly toward the far bank of the Cerfone. His horse finds its own way, and he is not aware of guiding it. He remains focused on the image he is continuing to construct for the chapel wall. He must protect the Virgin, reinforce the canopy with a padded fabric of great price, which will be held open by two angels whose harmonious, symmetrical gestures will accentuate the solidity and verticality of the woman standing in the center—hieratical and sovereign, and aware of that sovereignty, yet wearing on her face an expression of acceptance of what will come, and in her body a sign of her fragility. Piero must protect the Virgin in the space of the painting, while in real life he is obliged to abandon Silvia to the somber dance of death, forever childless, deprived of any possibility of being a source of a new life.

A bank of mist floats above the river, fragmenting the light into brilliant particles of softness. The village on the far bank is hidden from his gaze, as on the day they arrived, when he was observing the landscape as they left the forest. Everything around him has lost its consistency. The trees, the first houses, all the shapes he has known since childhood, are concealed as they melt into an indeterminate landscape of faded spots of color.

Things have become intangible, they are floating, all references have vanished: It is impossible to capture any contours with clarity, to determine any limits for a vanishing point, to elaborate a geometrical structure or establish any distance between oneself and the objects of the world. Piero's horse continues on its way, but the man on its back feels lost and disoriented, drowned in an imprecise light where all color has been dampened with softness, in a universe at the edge of dilution. When he reaches the other shore and the horse begins to climb, Piero notices a shape going in and out of the fog to his left, rising and falling, with the irregular motions of a butterfly. When the shape draws nearer, flying above him as if following him, Piero can see bursts of the pink and orange hues in the bird's plumage, and on its head a crown of flaming feathers. The bird flies on ahead, and gradually the fog begins to lift.

When Piero arrives at the house where Silvia is waiting for him, everything is sharp and clearly defined again: this clarity reassures him, but seems almost too abrupt, trenchant.

The moment he crosses the threshold, the strong and somewhat bitter odor assails him: it is the precious myrrh that Marta has been burning to purify the air and expel the miasma of death at work. Weeping has already taken over the household. Laid out on her bed, rigid, Silvia is breathing with great difficulty: Each expiration is marked by a moan from within, a hoarse rattle, and she does not seem to be breathing in. There is only a suspended moment where life is already departing. Her eyes never leave the ceiling, even when Piero places his hand, ever so gently, on her shoulder. She is trying to swallow, to open her mouth, to make a noise. He leans over toward her face, softly, as if not wishing to place any obstacles between her dying body and the air around it.

"The queen," murmurs Silvia, "the queen is expecting a child. It is a son, and he shall be king."

Immediately after Silvia's body was lowered into the earth, Piero shut himself away in Santa Maria di Momentana to be near where his wife is buried, in the little garden to the side of the chapel. He left Marta to assuage the villagers' fears regarding Silvia's illness—and his promises were upheld! The plague disappeared from the village after Silvia's funeral. Marta attributes the miracle to the powers of the fresco that Piero has begun. He has scarcely begun to design the preparatory drawings and already there are rumors about the Virgin to whom Piero has given Silvia's face, who is carrying the child to whom she never gave birth. Already women come to sit quietly in the chapel and murmur their litanies. The devotion they once reserved for the wooden statue of the Virgin and Child, the same image by which Piero's grandmother used to pray, has found a new object of fervor: the fresco is said to have the power to protect pregnant women until they give birth. Gradually, the rumor that has enveloped Monterchi spreads beyond the village; others talk about this painting that wards off misfortune from the village and protects the women who will bear its children.

Piero remains impervious to all the commotion. Alone now, he immerses himself in his work. He refuses any presence at his side. He has sent away the emissaries, who came to demand he return to the site of the work commissioned long ago in Arezzo and in Borgo, which have at last been delivered from the plague. In spite of their anger, Piero gave them no dates and no hope. He cannot even think about going away from this chapel, away from Silvia and his sacred task. His sole desire is to bring her to life for a second time, so that she might come into the light, into the world with the long-awaited child. The priest in charge of the offices at Santa Maria di Momentana who had used to come infrequently to the chapel, now comes every day, and protects Piero's work from the excessive fervor of the faithful and the pressing solicitations of his patrons. With the support of the bishop, who has been informed of the magnitude of the events, he has convinced the Franciscans in Arezzo and the Brotherhood of Mercy in Borgo to remain patient for a time. The offerings left at the Chapel of the Virgin have increased in such proportions that he can even envision sending them some compensatory funds.

When Fra Bartolomeo enters the chapel, he is obliged to negotiate for some time before he can reach the foot of the scaffolding where Piero is working. Piero hears nothing, and refuses to be disturbed; he is utterly absorbed by his study of minute details almost imperceptible to anyone viewing the painting from a distance. While Fra Bartolomeo stands at the foot of the altar, Piero is seeking to accentuate the harmony on the face of the Virgin by making her eyebrows thicker in their centerand narrower at the sides. He is using a tiny brush, in keeping with the infinitesimal range of his gestures. For a while Fra Bartolomeo respects his concentration and silence. He is moved to see Silvia again, as he knew her—serious, diligent, always concerned with doing what was right, and now so astonished to be with child that she cannot help but ascertain the reality of her condition with a gesture of her hand. And her gesture points out the object of her pride to all the women who made her suffer with their gossip.

How did she die? All through his own battle against the plague, which left him weak for a very long time, Bartolomeo wondered: Did Silvia return to the realm of the Father with some peace in her soul? Piero has depicted a certain sadness on her face: is this merely a sign of the painter's difficulty in accepting her disappearance? There is much that Fra Bartolomeo could reproach Silvia's husband with: how often has he confronted him about the harmful influence of the humanists? Through Piero's intermediary, they were in danger of preying upon Silvia's mind, of perverting her with the pernicious appeal of intellectual and material wealth, and with their scornful attitude toward simplicity. He was successful in his combat against the Roman project which—although Piero was not aware of this—went counter to the interests of the Franciscan order by serving those of Giovanni Bacci. But despite their differences and Piero's infidelities, Fra Bartolomeo respects the true, deep love of the painter for his wife. In no way did the monk betray his mission of protector and teacher as he guided the young woman through her duties as a wife—unusual ones at that, given a husband who was so out of the ordinary. Fra Bartolomeo protected Silvia, too, from the intrigue woven by the nobility around those artists who sought their favor. Silvia had a pure heart, which needed protection if the fragile dimension of the world's innocence was to be preserved in it.

Fra Bartolomeo had watched over Silvia from her childhood, saving her from herself, from any temptation that might have induced her to use her abilities elsewhere than in the service of God and mankind. She was not to know where she came from, at the risk of joining those who had preceded her in evil and murder. Her parents had set their city awash in blood before succumbing to an equally bloody vengeance. The uncle who had saved the child from death, from the blade of the cutthroats at the pay of the armed factions, had entrusted her, with a handsome sum of money, to the Franciscans. The complex terms of his will had one single purpose: the infernal cycle of reprisal must end with Silvia. Fra Bartolomeo had fulfilled that wish. Silvia died in such a saintly way that her image was now arousing the devotion of hundreds of the faithful. Her life and her very identity have been forgotten, she is nothing more than a model, a representation of the Virgin. Is this self-effacement not the best example for those who pray with piety before the mother of Christ, she who is prepared to offer her child for the salvation of the world?

Piero puts down his brush. He climbs down the scaffold with the stiff awkwardness of someone whose body has been forced into painful positions for hours on end. Incapable of seeing anything but his own painting, he fails to notice Fra Bartolomeo. The monk catches his attention by clearing his throat and walking back and forth with a heavy step; the Franciscan cowl is also not common, even in this place. When Piero recognizes his visitor his expression changes and becomes almost threatening and angry: "What are you doing here? Was her death not enough for you?"

"Do you think I am pleased by her death? Suffering is leading you astray, but I shall not hold it against you, I shall pray for you."

Piero holds back the words he would like to scream in reply. No, he will not tell to the monk to keep his prayers for himself. Yet those prayers did too little for Silvia; he can hardly want them for himself! But how can he surrender to such blasphemy: he must respect the men of God and preserve some respect for prayer.

"Silvia is no longer among us," continues Fra Bartolomeo. "So there is no longer any danger in revealing her origins. I thought it might be something of a relief for you to learn of her nobility."

"I am aware of her profound nobility. It is the only one that I care to keep the memory of. And as for the rest…we never needed to know when she was alive. Why do you want me to find out now? How might it be useful to me to preserve her image beyond her absence? She is noble, can you not see that?"

Fra Bartolomeo does not insist. To do so would only jeopardize the success of the mission with which his order, once again, has entrusted him.

"It will become even more apparent when you lend her features to the Queen of Sheba…on condition that you have that opportunity, and the time. Our brothers in Arezzo are eager to see the completion of the decoration of their church. They've already changed artists once, when Bicci di Lorenzo died. I am afraid they are prepared to revoke your contract should you delay further. That would be a pity; Silvia exhibited such wonderful talent as a storyteller, using the notes conveyed by our brother who had returned from the land of the infidels. Where then is the book she was still writing in on your last day in Borgo?"

"That is nothing to do with you, you have no need to know. I shall keep it preciously, with the few other things Silvia left behind. You have no right to anything which belonged to her."

"Don't be so certain of that, since you wish to know nothing of her origins nor of the conditions under which our order took her in! In any case, she wanted you to complete the frescoes of the chapel of the church of San Francesco d'Arezzo. You cannot leave this matter in doubt. So do not take too long!"

On leaving the chapel, Fra Bartolomeo takes one last glance at the finished fresco: with the two open panels, held by perfectly symmetrical angels, it unveils the image of the mother in all her humanity and greatness, admirable because she is only too aware of her future suffering, which she accepts. The love she commands is great, as her hand reaches gently toward the child protected by the folds of her blue gown.

Piero walks with a heavy step toward the small shed where he stores his tools and clothes. His intense dislike of Fra Bartolomeo has not changed. But the monk's strange conspiratorial manners do not prevent him from being right; Piero cannot deny the ties which Silvia had established with Bilqis.

At the back of the church the faithful are moving about; they have come to the church for very different reasons than those that have moved Piero to paint the fresco they venerate. He has been surpassed by the destiny of his work, and Silvia with him. They must go elsewhere, to seek exile from Monterchi yet again, and take the road—to Arezzo then, where the queen awaits, the queen who will not have Silvia's face, but a face created by Silvia. They have a great deal still, to do together.

About the Author

ALIETTE ARMEL lives in Paris, where she has been a critic for the *Magazine litteraire* since 1984. Trained as an historian, has pursued numerous other literary activities, including her 1997 biography of the French writer and ethnologist Michel Leiris. In 2000, she traveled to the Yemen to conduct research on the Queen of Sheba for this book. *Love, the Painter's Wife, and the Queen of Sheba* ("*Le voyage de Bilqîs*") was originally published in 2002 in France, where it was received with considerable critical acclaim. This is Armel's first novel.

The fonts used in this book are from the Garamond family.

The Toby Press Publishes fine fiction and is
available at bookstores everywhere. For more information,
please contact *The* Toby Press at www.tobypress.com.